CONTACT!

BY CRAIG DILOUIE

Crash Dive, Episode #1: Crash Dive

Crash Dive, Episode #2: Silent Running

Crash Dive, Episode #3: Battle Stations

Crash Dive, Episode #4: Contact!

Suffer the Children

The Retreat, Episode #1: Pandemic

The Retreat, Episode #2: Slaughterhouse

The Retreat, Episode #3: Die Laughing

The Retreat, Episode #4: Alamo

The Alchemists

The Infection

The Killing Floor

Children of God

Tooth and Nail

The Great Planet Robbery

Paranoia

CONTACT!

A NOVEL OF THE PACIFIC WAR

CRAIG DILOUIE

CONTACT!
A novel of the Pacific War
©2017 Craig DiLouie. All rights reserved.

This is a work of fiction. All characters and events portrayed in this novel are either fictitious or used fictitiously.

Editing by Timothy Johnson.
Cover art by Eloise Knapp Design.
Book layout by C. Marshall Publishing.

Published by ZING Communications, Inc.
www.CraigDiLouie.com

Area of operations. Saipan.

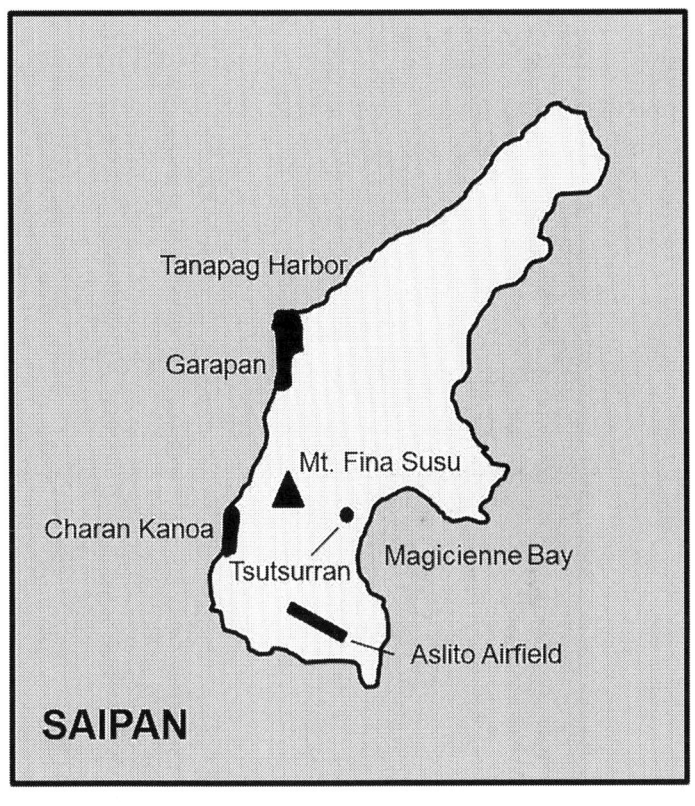

CHAPTER ONE
RUNAWAY TRAIN

On the *Sandtiger*'s bridge, Lt. Commander Charlie Harrison observed Captain Harvey conning her out of Pearl. Today, the fifteen-man Relief Crew 202 of the USS sea tender *Proteus* would determine if she was seaworthy.

They were healing, man and submarine, and getting to know each other again.

Seven months ago, *Sandtiger* limped into Pearl with new scars and a broom tied to her shears. Sailors crowded the wharf and watched in silence as the battered boat warped to the dock. Word had gotten around. Disaster in the Japan Sea. The sailors thought they were seeing a ghost ship, this sole survivor.

Then they'd cheered loud enough that ComSubPac heard it in his office.

Now, trailing black smoke, *Sandtiger* exited the harbor mouth for her shakedown. For Charlie, a moment of vertigo as she seemed to shrink against the vast Pacific.

Lt. Morrison said, "We're underway, Captain."

"Very well," Captain Harvey said. "Dismiss the maneuvering watch."

"Aye, aye."

"Set a course for two-seven-oh."

"Setting a course for two-seven-oh, aye," the first officer echoed.

Charlie smiled at the tedious but important routine. It felt like home just as being back at sea did.

The submarine's engines pulsed like a strong and healthy heartbeat as she found her bearing.

Sandtiger had survived, but it had been a near thing. Her wood decking and steel superstructure warped and broken. Commutator short circuits in the starboard main motor. The electrical and steering system turned fickle. Drain pump sparking. Multiple leaks, including one through the stern torpedo tubes.

Charlie had feared he'd see her scrapped, but she had gone straight to shore repairs. Struck by the loss of three fighting captains, ComSubPac wanted *Sandtiger* back in the thick of it. Vice Admiral Lockwood couldn't bring back Moreau, but he could honor the man's martial spirit.

The repairs had taken longer than expected. By the time the engineers declared her sea ready, Charlie had completed Prospective Commanding Officer (PCO) School in New London. He'd returned hopeful for a posting to new construction and had been happily surprised instead to find *Sandtiger* waiting for him.

He glanced over his shoulder at Waikiki Beach. A crowd of men stood on the white sands. The regular ship's company, wishing her the best. Somebody raised a drink in salute, probably Lt. Percy. Like Charlie, they belonged to her.

Charlie hoped to become her captain.

Ahead, the Pacific beckoned. The tropical sun burned across gentle swells, paving a golden road. A destroyer—the USS *Grant*, a four-gun Benham—emerged from the glare. Lt. Morrison called out the arrival of their escort.

Charlie beamed. Nothing could ruin this moment.

"Did you miss me, Mr. *Hara-kiri-san*?"

He started at the familiar grating voice. Looked up to see John Braddock, one of the four lookouts, grinning down at him from the shears.

"Keep your eyes on your sector," Charlie said on reflex.

He thought about the heavy thumping *Sandtiger* had taken on her last patrol. How good Braddock was at fixing equipment, even if he excelled at ruining everything else.

Charlie added, "And you know what, I actually did. What are you doing here?"

"Right now, I'm on lookout."

"I mean what are you doing on a relief crew?"

"Staying alive by staying as far away from you as possible, sir."

Just as Charlie remembered, Braddock made *sir* sound like *asshole*.

Captain Harvey lowered his binoculars and glanced up at the sailor before fixing Charlie with a glare. Charlie shut up and kept his eyes forward, his face a practiced mask of professional sullenness. Captain Squadron Commander Rich Cooper had said he could tag along but only if he stayed out of Harvey's way.

Lt. Morrison threw him a furtive wink. Brash and looking far too young to be first officer, he struck Charlie as a go-getter, chafing to transfer and see combat before the war ended. Stationed on sea tenders, relief crews manned submarines during shore repairs. They provided a valuable service but never faced the enemy.

Sandtiger continued to reach from the shore, making way on growling engines. The *Grant* paced her to starboard. Oahu's bright coastline and lush green mountains receded to a blur. The submarine's prow knifed the swells.

"Depth under the keel, 500 feet," Morrison said.

"Clear the topsides," the captain snarled.

The men hustled down the ladder to the conning tower. The last man called out he'd secured the hatch. The klaxon blasted twice as the captain gave the order to rig for dive. Wedged into a corner of the crowded room, Charlie listened to the boat's hum, felt it along his spine.

The iron lady appeared healthy and strong.

"Dive, dive, dive!"

"Maneuvering, Conn," Morrison said. "Stop the main engines. Switch to battery power."

The big generator, which powered the electric motors that turned *Sandtiger*'s four propellers, switched from engine to battery power.

"Rig out the bow planes."

The blades thumped as they extended into the sea.

"Manifold, close the main induction," the first officer continued.

The valve banged shut. The Christmas tree glowed green across the board, signifying all hull openings secured.

"Pressure in the boat, green board, Captain," Morrison said. "All compartments ready to dive."

Harvey scanned the conning tower, confirming everything was in order. Gaze settling on Charlie, he frowned. He clearly didn't like an officer from the regular ship's company being here. Probably felt he could give the boat her proper shakedown without some hotshot looking over his shoulder.

"Very well," the captain said. "Planes, take us to ninety feet."

The brawny planesmen turned their wheels in opposite directions. Bow planes rigged to dive, stern planes angling the submarine.

Morrison: "Control, open all main vents."

The manifoldmen opened the vents to flood the ballast tanks with seawater, draining the boat's buoyancy.

Harvey would dive in stages to the boat's test depth, checking her trim and hull integrity. After that, steep ascents and descents to give her a thorough trial. Angles and dangles. Then he'd fire dummy torpedoes at the *Grant*.

The men leaned as *Sandtiger* tilted for her dive.

Charlie stiffened. Something was wrong.

The deck kept tilting.

Sandtiger surged forward at a steep down angle and plummeted into the depths.

"Control your planes!" Harvey cried in surprise.

A wrench clattered down the sloping deck. Charlie gripped a handhold, watching the captain. Harvey grimaced as he tried to figure out the problem.

"Passing ninety feet!" Morrison said, his brashness gone.

Out of control, *Sandtiger* bolted toward the bottom like a runaway train. The depth gauge needle spun crazily as she sank.

"Passing 150 feet!"

"Recommend blowing the ballast tanks!" Charlie called out.

Harvey glanced around wildly, saying nothing.

"Blow the goddamn tanks, Captain! All back emergency!"

The captain gave him a blank stare, his face glistening with sweat.

"Now or we're done, Captain!"

"Passing 200 feet!"

The boat trembled as she hurtled toward her test depth.

"Surface, surface, surface!" Morrison screamed.

The first officer had taken the conn without declaring

he was doing so. The desperate crew obeyed without question.

The helmsman yanked the alarm handle. "Surfacing, aye!"

"Control, blow the main ballast tanks!"

Harvey snapped out of his funk and bellowed, "Hard rise on the bow and stern planes! All back emergency!"

"Aye, aye!"

All eyes were on the captain now, while he stared at the depth gauge.

"Passing 300 feet!"

The orders came too late. *Sandtiger* was passing her test depth and entering pressures that could warp her steel hull.

Then deeper until the heavy waters crushed her like an egg.

Harvey shouted fresh commands to pump water from the amidships trim tank out to sea. The boat shook as her engines fought to check her descent.

Depth, 350—

The hull groaned and popped as the surrounding water pressed against it.

Charlie's mind flashed to the Japan Sea. Nixon laboring to close a spraying valve with a pipe wrench. Liebold dragging a body through the brackish water covering the deck. Percy screaming into the 7MC.

Evie standing at the edge of a pier at Mare Island, waving a red scarf.

Four hundred feet.

Sandtiger shuddered as if she were coming apart—

Then Charlie felt the change.

The boat's descent was slowing. No longer sinking like a rock.

Manifold had punched a bubble into the bow and main ballast tanks. The deck began to level out as the bow rose.

Sandtiger lurched again and shot up fifty feet. The crew worked hard to get her under control and keep her moving toward the surface.

Morrison took a ragged breath. "We're out of it, Captain."

"Something's wrong with this boat," Harvey growled.

He glared at the submarine that had flatfooted him. Scanned its dials and levers as if this mere inspection might derive the cause among thousands of moving parts.

His glare settled on Charlie as if he'd found his culprit.

Charlie didn't care. He'd just survived another brush with death; the captain's embarrassment and anger meant nothing to him. He had a bigger concern.

What was wrong with *Sandtiger*?

CHAPTER TWO
THE SOUVENIR

The USS *Sandtiger* lay moored next to *Proteus*, whose crew swarmed the submarine's innards searching for the malfunction.

In three hours, Charlie would meet with the squadron commander. He chipped in to pull apart the hydraulic system in the control room.

The auxiliarymen noticed the oak leaf pinned to his service khakis but thought nothing of it. On the submarines, officers and crew worked alongside each other to do what needed doing.

The men labored shirtless in the sweltering heat. Charlie took off his own shirt and hung it from an overhead valve. The men glanced at the pale scars that ran like lightning down his ribs.

"*Hara-kiri*," one murmured, nudging his mates.

Focused on his task, Charlie ignored them. He'd pictured walking into Cooper's office and reporting a clean bill of health for the boat. Then Cooper would give him command along with choice hunting grounds for his next patrol.

Right now, that fantasy wasn't looking likely.

Submarines dove and surfaced based on buoyancy. At the order to submerge, a crewman pulled levers on a manifold. Pressurized hydraulic fluid shot down tubes to pistons. The pistons opened vents at the top of ballast tanks filled with high-pressure air. As the air escaped, seawater flooded the tank via ports at its bottom.

The bow tanks flooded first, next the amidships tanks, finally the after tanks, resulting in a controlled forward descent. Air made the submarine lighter, water heavier. As the submarine's weight exceeded that of the seawater it displaced, it gained negative buoyancy and dived. A simple principle, though controlling it required a complex hydraulic system running the length of the ship.

"Commander," a voice said behind him. "May I have a word?"

Captain Harvey probably wanted to talk to him about the system failure. Charlie didn't want to discuss the man's handling of the emergency. Men made mistakes, and he hoped Harvey had learned from his. Charlie would make nothing of it.

"Of course, Captain," he said.

He followed the man into the passageway. Two grease monkeys squeezed past toward the control room.

Harvey grinned and said, "Get off my fucking boat."

Charlie wiped his oily hands on a rag to hide his rising anger. Right or wrong, Harvey commanded the *Sandtiger*. His word was law.

"I'll go ashore at once, Captain."

"Very well."

Thirty minutes until his meeting with Cooper, and still he had no idea what caused *Sandtiger*'s nosedive.

"Captain?"

"Yes. What is it?"

Charlie said, "It's *my* fucking boat, and I expect you to take care of her."

He found his shirt and black tie in the control room. The shirt had fallen onto the deck. Streaked with grease, his pants looked no better. He stuffed the tie into his pocket and checked his watch again. He had just enough time to return to his quarters and change before his meeting.

He paused at the ladder that would take him up into the conning tower and, above that, the bridge and open air. He'd missed something.

He said, "Hey, Chief."

The chief of the boat looked up from his work. "Commander?"

"Where's John Braddock?"

"He went aft, sir. Said he had a theory."

Charlie released the rung and hurried through the crew's mess and quarters. Through the engine room, which was like walking between giant locomotives. Into the maneuvering room with its dizzying array of levers, dials, and gauges. Then the aft torpedo room and its rack of unfired dummy torpedoes.

Part of the deck was gone, the metal plates piled next to the hole alongside scattered tools. Braddock worked alone, head and torso buried in *Sandtiger*'s machinery, ass in the air.

"What are you doing, Braddock?"

"Fixing your boat, sir." His hairy hand emerged. "Angled wrench."

Charlie picked up the heavy tool and placed it in the hand, which retreated back into the hole.

Main ballast tank number seven was below this part of the deck. The last in line to fill during a dive. He followed Braddock's theory. If the tank didn't flood, the bow would become heavy while the stern remained buoyant, resulting in a nosedive.

"You think the main vents are stuck closed," he said.

If the vents stuck, the compressed air couldn't escape. And water, acting on the upward pressure from the sea, couldn't surge into the tank and make it heavy.

"I know they're stuck. I'm trying to unstick them." Braddock's hand returned. "Screwdriver."

Charlie gave it to him. "A problem in the hydraulics was more likely."

"I had a hunch."

"So why won't it open?"

The big machinist didn't answer, grunting as he labored. Then he emerged, his barrel chest splattered with oil. "Looks like you brought home a souvenir, sir."

He held out a chunk of crumpled steel. Debris from

a sinking ship that found its way into the submarine. Charlie took it and felt its weight. He remembered the destroyer's sound as it broke up in the depths. Like nails on a chalkboard, thousands of them, played at the volume of a scream.

Braddock said, "Just like the Japs. Even after they sink, they try to kill you."

"What are you doing on a relief crew?"

Recent graduates from Submarine School comprised relief crews. Not experienced seamen like John Braddock.

"I thought I already answered that, sir."

"Come on, Braddock. You're too good for this. We need men like you."

"You need guys like me so you can take crazy chances getting what you want. The war's almost over. I aim to survive it and guys like you."

Charlie shook his head and stood to leave. "Forget it."

"I did my part," the man called after him. "Sir."

Confounded as usual by the machinist's ability to irritate and impress him at the same time, Charlie didn't respond. In any case, he couldn't linger.

He now had fifteen minutes until his meeting with Cooper. Just enough time to make it, but not enough to change his uniform. The meeting was going to be a lot different than he'd imagined.

At least he had an answer as to why *Sandtiger* had failed and gone out of control. That had to be worth far more than showing up in clean khakis.

CHAPTER THREE

THE STRANGERS

Charlie mounted to the bridge. *Proteus* loomed next to *Sandtiger*. To starboard, more tenders and submarines lay moored. One had been gutted, its electrical wiring snaking across the pier. In bright sunshine, sailors sat on a bench dangling over the side, repainting the hull. Cleaned after months of hot-bunking, mattresses dried on a clothesline. A rivet gun chattered.

A gang of disheveled men stood on the distant wharf. Five lean and hungry soldiers in Army green. Patched, grimy camouflage uniforms. They looked like they'd walked straight off some Pacific battlefield. They eyed *Sandtiger* like deserters hoping she'd take them to some tropical island far from the war.

Still pale, Morrison greeted him on the main deck.

"I was hoping I'd be tested," the man said. "Careful what you wish for, right?"

"You did fine. In fact, you saved our lives."

"Then why do I feel so lousy?"

"That's the thing about being tested. You never quite believe you passed."

"Something like that, yeah," Morrison said.

"That and you start thinking about how nuts you were to chase the test in the first place."

The young lieutenant smiled. "I did, in fact, wonder what the hell I'm doing here instead of staying back home, making money and babies."

Charlie handed him the gnarled scrap of metal. "Braddock found your problem. This was clogging the vents in the aft main ballast tank."

"Wow, is this …?"

"A shard from the hull of a Japanese destroyer we sank."

"Wow."

Morrison eyed it with wonder, no doubt imagining new tests to face, all thoughts of making money and babies banished.

Not Charlie. He shivered at the sight of it as if it were haunted.

After the Battle of La Pérouse Strait, *Sandtiger*'s crew labored to keep her running across the Pacific. Fearing the next dive might be their last, Charlie ordered most of the trip made on the surface. He'd remembered how the S-55 sank just outside Cairns with her battle flags streaming. Sometimes, a captain chose to go down with his ship. Other times, though, a ship chose to go down with her captain.

After everything he'd survived, that little piece of debris nearly killed him. One little thing jamming the works of an otherwise flawless fighting machine. That was all it took to disable and send it careening toward the bottom.

It could make a man superstitious. Take what Braddock said seriously. That the Japanese sailors he'd killed were still trying to take him with them.

"Keep it," Charlie said. "I don't want it."

"Hey, thanks!"

"I have to get to a meeting. Good luck to you. A word of advice …"

"Sure."

"Stay out of Captain Harvey's way a while. Let him cool off."

Morrison had essentially taken command during the crisis. Though he'd saved the boat and the lives of all aboard, a captain could call it mutiny. It was no small thing, taking command from a ship's captain.

"That's good advice. Thank you, Commander."

"Good luck to you," Charlie said.

The sailor on gangway watch saluted as he passed. He returned it. As he reached the wharf, the ratty soldiers shifted their gaze to him.

"How many men you killed?" one called out to him.

Charlie paused, evaluating them in their patched fatigues. They were all bronzed by the tropical sun. They hadn't shaved in days. Rangy jungle fighters who exuded menace. Most notable was their long stare, like drivers always keeping one eye in the rearview.

One eye always reliving the past, and surviving it. Charlie knew that look well. He saw it often enough in the mirror.

He ignored the soldier who'd spoken to him and focused on the man standing in front, whose mouth curled into a grin. No visible insignia indicating rank, but clearly the gang's leader.

"You're Harrison, ain't you?" He spoke with a combination of southern drawl and twang.

"That's right," Charlie said.

"So how many?" the other soldier asked again.

Was he kidding?

He said, "Who's asking?"

"I'm asking."

"Then none of your business." Charlie kept walking.

He spared a glance over his shoulder. The leader's smile widened, and he nodded. Charlie turned away, bewildered. He had a feeling he'd passed some sort of test but had no idea what it was.

Turning the corner, he stopped and bent, hands on his knees. Legs turned to jelly. The stress of *Sandtiger*'s sudden plummet had finally caught up to him. He leaned against a wall trembling until it subsided, the strange soldiers forgotten.

The shakes didn't bother him. They meant he was normal, human. They meant he hadn't grown used to facing death. He hoped he never would.

CHAPTER FOUR
A NEW CAPTAIN

Covered in a film of grease and sweat, Charlie knocked on the doorway of Captain Squadron Commander Rich Cooper's office. Framed by wood paneling and gray file cabinets, the grizzled officer beckoned from his desk.

Two officers sat in chairs with their backs to him. Charlie glimpsed naval insignia. A lieutenant and a lieutenant-commander, one slim, the other heavyset.

"Lt. Commander Charles Harrison," he said. "Reporting to the squadron commander as ordered."

Cooper gave him a once-over. "You get run over by a truck, Harrison?"

"A Jap destroyer to be precise, sir."

"I hope you gave him more than you got."

One of the seated men guffawed. "Are you kidding? Our man Harrison can't cross the street without sinking something."

Charlie started at the familiar voice. "Rusty!"

His old friend rose and offered his hand. "Hi-de-ho, brother."

Charlie grabbed and shook it. "Great to see you."

"Same to you. I'm off submarines. I work for Captain Voge in operations now. Naval intelligence to be exact. That's why I'm here. I just got in from Melbourne."

He couldn't stop grinning at Rusty's lopsided smile. "Damn." He glanced at Cooper and added, "We served together on the 55 in the Solomons. Back in '42."

"A lifetime ago," Rusty said. "I taught this cowboy everything he knows."

His friend seemed much older now, which made Charlie think about how he'd also aged much in the past twenty months. They weren't boys anymore.

"Tell us about this destroyer," Cooper said.

"The one that almost sank you," Rusty said.

"How did you hear about that?"

His friend tapped his forehead. "Naval intelligence."

"*Sandtiger* nosed down on her first dive," Charlie explained. "Lt. Morrison took the conn and got us out of it. I pitched in with the A-gangers to find out what happened. Turns out a piece of a destroyer we sank in the Japan Sea got stuck in the vents of the number seven main ballast tank."

He'd said, *we sank*, not *I sank*, though he'd been in command at the time. Charlie made a point always to use *we* when claiming accomplishments and *I* when taking responsibility for failures. Giving credit and blame where it was due.

"That'll do it," the other seated man said. "Send you to the bottom like a rock."

The lieutenant-commander stood, offering Charlie a good look at the man. He smiled at Charlie with a round face perched atop a slightly stooped and rotund body. Then he held out his big hand to shake.

Cooper said, "Harrison, this is Lt. Commander Howard Saunders. He'll be joining you on your next war patrol." He cleared his throat. "As *Sandtiger*'s new skipper."

Charlie kept his face neutral while his gut took a nosedive. He found himself shaking the man's beefy paw. "Pleased to meet you, sir."

He knew Saunders by reputation. Captain of the *Flagfin*. A long-timer in the submarines—nine war patrols, 39,000 tons of Japanese shipping sent to the bottom. On his last patrol, a Japanese seaplane caught his boat out in the open and strafed it. He spent five months in a hospital from bullet wounds while another man took *Flagfin* out on patrol to the murky but shallow waters of the Yellow Sea, named for Gobi Desert sands blowing east and turning its surface golden. There, the Japanese sank her with all hands aboard.

"You've done a hell of a job for the submarines," Saunders said warmly, though his eyes sized Charlie up.

"Thank you, sir," Charlie said, sizing up the captain right back.

"Cooper isn't finished, Charlie," Rusty said. "Hear him out."

"I didn't say a word!"

"I served with you in combat. I always know what you're thinking."

Cooper said, "This is Howard's last patrol. He'll be in command, but he'll also be mentoring you to take over. You'll be PCO on this patrol."

After surviving the Sea of Japan, Charlie's violent career in the submarines had reached the doorstep of its ultimate goal—command of his own boat. Cooper had more or less promised him that, but something had changed.

While he'd hoped for command, he held a stoic view of the Navy, which operated on a grand and often obtuse logic. There was no point fighting it and no hard feelings. He stayed focused on his main goal, which was playing a part in defeating the Japanese and ending the war. He'd be going out on this patrol as prospective commanding officer, which might afford more responsibilities and a chance to learn from a seasoned veteran.

And after that, finally, he'd get command. If Cooper kept his promise.

"As long as we get good hunting grounds, I'll be happy," he said.

The men smiled at that.

"We'll get along just fine," Saunders said.

"Is your boat ready to sail?" Cooper asked Charlie.

"Harvey has to take her out again and give her tubes a workout. Otherwise, she's ready for sea. We're still missing an officer, though."

Jack Liebold had quit the submarines. He'd sucked in too much chlorine gas aboard *Sabertooth*. Right now, he was convalescing stateside. He'd left happy, though. So drunk after his good-bye party the stewardesses had to drag him up the stairs into the plane. He'd done a lot of good in the war. And he had his own stories to tell now.

"Yes, I received your requests about it," the squadron commander said.

"I'd be happy to recommend Morrison for the job," he told Saunders. "He can think in a crisis, and he's chomping at the bit for a chance to get in the war."

"We already have a man in mind," Cooper said. "Get your boat ready for sea. The patrol briefing is in three days. You're going back to the war."

"Aye, aye, sir. I'll get on it right away."

"Not right away," Rusty said. "First, you're gonna let me buy you a drink at the O-Club so we can catch up."

CHAPTER FIVE
POST-CONCUSSION

They found an empty booth in the Officer's Club at the Royal Hawaiian Hotel and ordered scotch on the rocks. Charlie spotted a nearby table where Mush Morton, then captain of a V-boat, once raised his glass to him.

Rusty: "Penny for your thoughts?"

Morton had gone on to command the *Wahoo* and blaze new submarine doctrine summarized by his well-known motto, "Stay with the bastard till he's on the bottom!" Moreau, Rickard, and Shelby had all taken inspiration from him.

Now these old submarine aces were gone, and new fighting captains had taken their place. Thanks to men like O'Kane, Dealey, Coye, Triebel, Gross, and Saunders, the submarines had begun achieving spectacular successes in the war.

"Just thinking about somebody I admire," Charlie said.

Their drinks arrived.

Rusty raised his glass. "To us being here."

"And to everybody who isn't."

They drank.

"So how are you, brother?" Rusty said.

Charlie closed his eyes to savor the whiskey burning down his gullet. He'd made a rule to drink socially, and only rarely, but he enjoyed it when he did. Enjoyed it a bit too much lately.

His instincts told him his friend was still working.

"Is it you asking or Navy Intelligence?"

Rusty laughed. "Both, since we're being honest."

"My honest answer is I'm fit for duty."

"Post-concussion syndrome. That's what the fitness report says."

The Battle of La Pérouse Strait had given him twenty-one stitches, battered ribs, and a swollen knee. Another Purple Heart. While attending PCO School, however, he began to suffer bouts of dizziness, mental fog, and depression.

The doctors diagnosed him with post-concussion syndrome. The delayed result of the head injury he'd suffered during the battle. No treatment. It would go away on its own, or it wouldn't.

"That's what it says," Charlie echoed.

"What do you think?"

He decided to keep being honest. "I think my problem might be worse than that."

Rusty set his glass down. "What do you mean?"

"My problem might be peace."

Charlie wondered whether he now served only one purpose. Like the submarines he watched depart on their missions.

Rusty sat back with a sigh. "You remember Reynolds."

The S-55's XO knew that, even if he survived the war, he could never go home. Charlie wasn't thinking about him, though. He was remembering Evie's warning not to give too much of himself to the war. She said he'd married it. She didn't understand. You didn't always have a choice. The war had a way of taking whether you gave or not. Sometimes, the old girl married you.

"I don't remember much of it," Charlie said. "The battle in the strait. It comes back to me in flashes, triggered by loud noises or the smell of diesel oil. The way you remember a bad dream."

The deck plates buckling under his feet. Brackish water pouring into the conning tower. Men screaming in the darkness.

Only in his dreams did he remember everything.

"How are you getting along with it?" Rusty said. Gone was the veneer of a naval intelligence officer. He was asking as a friend.

"I'm getting better on the harmonica. That and I get letters from Evie that keep me tethered to home. Plus the busywork Cooper gives me and time spent in the attack trainer, which is every chance I get. Is this why he didn't give me the job?"

"Maybe. I don't know. It could be Saunders wanted

one more dance, and Cooper felt the Navy owed it to him."

Charlie finished his scotch and set the glass down. "I'm fit for the job."

While disappointed at Cooper's change of heart, he had to admit he'd felt something else. Relief. He'd returned from the Sea of Japan as beaten up inside and out as the *Sandtiger*. PCO School and long months spent warming the bench hadn't helped. He believed returning to the war would set him straight. He wasn't sure, however, that he was ready for the intense pressures of commanding a boat.

Careful what you wish for, Morrison had said. Damned straight. He wanted to command. When he told Rusty he was fit for the job, he'd told the truth. Still, he wondered if he was truly ready. The Japanese debris in the after ballast tank had shaken him. One little thing could destroy a boat. One little thing jamming a vent or one little thing a captain misses in the heat of combat.

"I believe you're fit," Rusty said. "Your teachers gave you top marks in your classes and the attack trainer. Whatever's been eating you, it didn't affect your performance. And during the nosedive today, what happened? What did you do?"

"Harvey froze. I told him to blow the ballast tanks and go all back full, but he hesitated. If Morrison hadn't taken the conn, I would have. It was a close one."

"I believe you on that too. You're being too hard on

yourself. You earned your oak leaf the hard way, and you sound fit to me. In fact, I recommended *Sandtiger* for this mission because I thought you'd be in command."

"Then what's got Navy Intelligence so interested in me all of a sudden?"

"Right now, Captain Saunders."

"What about him?"

"Between you and me, I think he's had it. He's been through the wringer."

"Oh, for God's sake."

"That makes me interested in you. If he loses it, somebody will need to pick up the ball and get the mission done."

"Just let me get back to fighting the Japanese," Charlie groaned. "At least with them, I know where things stand."

Rusty waved at the waitress and ordered another round. Charlie scanned the busy club. A musician played a ukulele in the corner, though one barely heard the music over the hubbub of gossiping officers. The red light and cigarette smoke reminded him once again of the S-55, rigged for red and getting a pounding.

He spotted Percy and Nixon at a table across the room. Percy regaled a small crowd of young officers, who listened riveted to some tall tale. Nixon sat with a single unfinished bottle in front of him, set there like a stage prop.

"One more drink," Charlie said. "Then I have to get the boat ready."

He was worried about the crew. Half shanghaied to feed new construction, replaced by greenhorns fresh from Submarine School. The rest idle so long they needed retraining. And no time for it. They sailed at the end of the week.

A beat-up submarine, a crew gone soft, and a captain who'd lost his edge. They were still missing an officer. God, what a mess. They'd have to drill all the way across the Pacific and hope to regain some semblance of combat efficiency.

When the drinks arrived, he resisted the urge to slam it back. He took a single sip instead and set it down with care.

"So where are we going, anyway?" he asked.

"Sorry, brother," Rusty said. "That's top secret until the briefing."

"We're taking commandos into Japanese territory."

His friend sprayed scotch and wiped his mouth. "What makes you say that?"

Those soldiers had been interested in *Sandtiger* for a reason. Just a guess, but Rusty's reaction confirmed it. It explained why Rusty had been in Melbourne.

MacArthur and his USAFFE headquarters operated out of Melbourne. The famous general wanted boots on the ground somewhere in the Pacific, probably the Philippines. *Sandtiger* would get them there.

Charlie tapped his head. "Naval intelligence."

"Well, don't go speculating to anybody else. I could get in a lot of trouble."

Playing taxi didn't sound too dangerous. Then again, the last time he'd given a ferry ride, he'd fought an aircraft carrier.

"This mission," Rusty added, "is one of the most important of the war. That's why I'll be coming along with you."

"You're our replacement officer!"

"Look at you. For once, I get to surprise you. Putting this op together took a lot of doing. I'm coming to make sure it all goes right. I've also gotten itchy on dry land. I think the war will be over soon. A year tops. I'd like to be there at the end."

"You an optimist," Charlie said. "I never thought I'd see the day. That or this op is so big you really believe it's the start of the end of the war."

"What did I tell you about speculating? What I can say is my son is three years old now, growing up without his daddy. I want this goddamn war to end, and soon."

Charlie raised his glass to that, and they drank. "So it looks like we're serving together again."

"I told you we someday would."

"Seeing as we're in the same boat, I'd like to ask you a favor."

CHAPTER SIX
HOTEL STREET

Charlie and Rusty crossed the room and approached Nixon, blinking at his shouting companions. The conversation died as Charlie approached. The red-faced officers stared at him and nudged each other.

"Hello, Exec," the engineering officer said. "Haven't seen you in a while." The man's head tilted. "Nineteen days, to be exact."

"We're back in action," Charlie told him. "We sail in five days."

"Yes, I just got the word."

The scuttlebutt traveled fast. He didn't mind, as it would help him round up *Sandtiger*'s wayward children.

"Plenty to get done," Nixon added. "Final checks, stores, trim calculations—"

"Plenty," Charlie agreed. "This is Lt. Rusty Grady. He's replacing Liebold."

Nixon looked up at Rusty with a pained expression.

"Nice to meet you," said Rusty, warned about the engineering officer's social awkwardness.

"Where's Percy?" Charlie asked him.

"The moment he heard, he ran off to Hotel Street."

"The crew's gone soft," he told Rusty. "Come on, Nixon. Let's go."

If he didn't track down Percy, the man would go on a tear and show up drunk as the boat was disembarking.

"Sure," said Nixon, grateful for the excuse to leave and get back to work.

"Give 'em hell, *Hara-kiri*," one of the officers said. His comrades cheered, clashing their bottles.

As they left the club, Rusty smirked and said, "*Hara-kiri*. Isn't that what John Braddock called you after you almost took a dip in the Coral Sea?"

"Stuff it, Rusty."

"You're not that guy anymore," Rusty observed. "Yet you are."

They walked out of the pink concrete stucco Royal Hawaiian with its Moorish architecture. The wide and sandy beach stretched to the brilliant blue water. Sailors lay on blankets and swam with the rollers, the luckier ones accompanied by bikini-clad Hawaiian girls. A destroyer and a minesweeper steamed offshore, a stern reminder all fun was temporary.

Nixon pointed. "There's Chief Petty Officer McDonough."

Smokey sprawled in the shade of a palm tree. Nearby, a concertina-wire barrier segregated the beach from the adjacent beachfront, which was open to civilians. Hands clasped on his chest and an old cowboy hat covering his face, he lay stretched out next to a neat pyramid of empty Pabst Blue Ribbon cans.

Charlie nudged him with his foot. Smokey growled and pushed up the brim of his hat.

"Thought you might be dead," Charlie said.

The quartermaster grinned at the inside joke. "I heard you might be."

"Close but no cigar." Charlie pointed. "Is that the chief?"

Chief of the Boat Spike Sullivan sat cross-legged on the sand near the surf's edge. A bronzed giant in shorts and sunglasses, still as a statue.

"He's meditating," Smokey explained. "Learned it from the Jap prisoner we shot. Said it keeps him calm."

A strange habit for a sailor, but one didn't begrudge Spike anything. The man stood six-three and weighed two-twenty.

"So what's the dope, Exec?" the quartermaster said.

"You can start rounding up the boys. They've been at liberty long enough. Tell them we sail in five days. No time for retraining. We're going to hit the ground running and drill all the way out there."

"Sounds fine."

Charlie glanced at Rusty. "Navy Intelligence has a big one for us."

"Sounds fine," Smokey repeated. He was just happy to get back to sea.

They left him to continue their search for Percy. After a short visit to Charlie's room so he could change, they caught a bus into downtown Honolulu.

Military police everywhere. Hawaii was still under martial law, ruled by Lt. General Emmons. The Hawaiian Department controlled the newspapers, limited telephone calls to the mainland, and imposed curfews and blackouts. It interned people of Japanese descent, censored all outgoing mail, and confiscated land. The Department even issued special currency, rendered void if the islands fell to the Japanese. The military had turned Hawaii into a fortress.

Charlie and his comrades got off in Chinatown. Long lines of servicemen wrapped around the block. Old Chinese ladies laughed at the sailors from beauty parlors and second-floor apartment windows. Shoeshine boys joked with them. Local women walked past carrying boxes of empty milk bottles. A small boy crossed the street with a gas mask swinging from his hip.

Hands thrust in their pockets, the sailors fidgeted in the bright sun. Keeping an eye on things, military police sweated in their helmets.

Hotel Street meant one thing, and that was prostitutes.

Living in a collection of brothels scattered among other businesses, some 200 women did a lively trade, charging $3 for three minutes. Assembly-line sex on a bullpen system. Matrons lingered outside the boogie houses, eyeing the customers and weeding out the drunks. Inside, the man paid his fee, received a poker chip, and entered a cubicle where he undressed. The prostitute came in, inspected him for VD, and serviced him before moving on to the next room.

Despite being illegal, the Hawaiian Department sanctioned it, seeing it as good for morale. And by regulating it, they reduced VD, a big concern for the military because it depleted manpower available for the war.

"Somebody told me each girl works twenty days a month and has a quota of 100 men a day," Nixon said. "The girl keeps $2. That's $48,000 a year."

Rusty whistled. "I'm in the wrong profession."

"Five hours a day of it," Nixon noted.

"Hardly pennies from heaven," Charlie said. "I'd rather earn my pay being depth-charged."

"Most came over from San Francisco," Nixon added. "Work for six months and then go home with their earnings."

"You seem to know a lot about it," said Rusty.

Nixon nodded happily. "I intend to go into business after the war."

"Not a brothel, I hope."

"No, no," the engineering officer stammered. "But it's an interesting model."

Charlie eyed the buildings and felt the old curiosity about what it'd be like to touch a woman again, even if it was only for the briefest time. He found the idea exciting and thought about it more often than he'd admit, but he was too prudish to do it. Despite his urges, releasing into a stranger after three minutes wasn't a great time. The reality probably didn't stack up against the idea.

Best to focus on getting Sandtiger *ready for war*, Charlie thought. After the war ended, he'd have all the time in the world to think about women.

"It's going to take forever to find him in this crowd," Rusty said.

He pointed. "There's our man."

Hard to miss Percy with his loud Aloha shirts.

The communications officer swayed on his feet, sweating booze. Charlie reached to hold him steady.

"Unhand me," Percy cried. "I'm a decorated war hero."

"Actually, it was a unit citation," Nixon said.

"Either way, I don't want to go back. I'm staying right here on active duty."

"We sail in five days," Charlie said. "We have a lot of work to prepare *Sandtiger* for her patrol. We need to get started by tomorrow."

"Tomorrow! Who cares about tomorrow?" Percy pointed at the brothel in front of him. "My first time at the Bronx. They have Hawaiian and Japanese girls. I'm gonna cross something off my list of things to do before I die."

"Penetrate Japanese hooker," Rusty said. "That just leaves climbing Everest."

Percy scowled at him.

"This is Rusty Grady," Charlie said. "He'll be replacing Liebold. I served with him on the 55."

"There's only room for one funny man on this boat," Percy growled.

"You're still the champion," Rusty assured him.

"What about an instrument? You play one?"

"The fiddle, though I'm not too good with it."

The communications officer's face went red. Charlie stiffened, ready to jump between the two men.

"Christ, why didn't you say so?" Percy exploded. "I taught Harrison here the harmonica. I play banjo. Man, we are gonna jam!"

"The boat, Percy," Charlie said. "Let's go."

"Come on, Exec," the man begged. "One last hurrah."

"At this rate, it'll be curfew before you get in there."

"The line's not moving at all," Nixon said.

The matron came out and waved her arms. "No more! Go home!"

The servicemen grumbled. Some shouted questions and abuse. A moment later, a line of women left the brothel carrying signs. The sailors erupted in catcalls and wolf whistles.

"Hey, baby doll," a sailor called out. "What gives?"

The woman struck a sultry pose and raised her sign. "We're on strike, sailor!"

The crowd roared in surprise at the news.

"Interesting," Nixon said. "The military fixes the

price, so it must be the working conditions. They can't live anywhere else in the town. They can't even leave the district. Maybe they want some changes."

"Hookers of the world unite," Rusty said.

"Just my rotten luck," Percy groaned.

The brothels were all emptying. Two hundred women marched toward the police station, just a few blocks away.

"I'll be there, Exec," Percy shouted over the confusion.

"What?"

"Remember I said you got to hang loose in the submarines? Well, you also have to get your kicks while you can. I always have a backup plan."

"We're with you girls!" a sailor cried. "Come on, boys!"

A mob of servicemen surged after the women, cheering them on while the MPs blew their whistles. Roaring sailors pushed past them.

"We'd better make tracks," Rusty said. "This could get ugly."

"You're right about that," Charlie said. "Percy—"

The communications officer had disappeared.

CHAPTER SEVEN
HIGH TIDE

Three days later, Charlie entered the briefing room and set his peaked cap next to several others on a side table. Exhausted from preparing *Sandtiger*, he felt confident she would be ready to sail on schedule. Scattered all over island deep in liberty, the crew heard the call and returned to base. Still no Lt. Percy, though. Charlie knew the lieutenant would keep his promise and show up for the loadout. Still, Charlie planned to give the man hell.

In the corner, Saunders spoke to Cooper and Rusty in a quiet but urgent tone that didn't invite interruption. Charlie studied his new commander from across the room. The captain's record spoke of being aggressive in pursuit and cool under fire. If not an artist in combat, a very capable technician.

The scuttlebutt told another story. During his last two patrols, Saunders had become unpredictable. He'd start an approach cool and methodical only to suddenly veer into reckless shortcuts. One of these resulted in *Flagfin* strafed by a Japanese plane. No wonder Rusty was worried.

Nine patrols, a lot for a commander. ComSubPac typically pulled captains off the line after five. The intense pressures wore a man down. Saunders apparently had enough clout to go the full nine. This patrol would be his tenth time out.

"Coffee, Commander?"

Charlie turned toward the only other man in the room, an Army officer in dress uniform.

"Thank you." He accepted the mug. "You clean up well."

"You too. Last time I saw you, you were covered in engine grease."

"I had a feeling we'd be meeting again."

The man smiled and extended his hand. "Lt. Jonas Cotten," he drawled. "Sixth Army Special Reconnaissance Unit, Alamo Scouts."

Charlie shook it. "Lt. Commander Charlie Harrison, XO of the *Sandtiger*. You guys have an odd way of introducing yourselves."

"Singer always does that. He likes to test anybody we'll be working with."

"I understand it was a test. I just don't see the point of it."

"The point ain't the answer; it's how the man answers," Cotten explained. "If it matters to you, you passed with flying colors."

"I'm wondering why it matters to you. I'm not the captain."

"So I hear." The sergeant's eyes shifted to Saunders. "What kind of man is he?"

"I don't know yet, Lieutenant," Charlie said. "I haven't served with him. But his record says he's one of our best."

"Call me Jonas. We Scouts are an informal bunch."

The pow-wow broke up. The men grabbed chairs around the gleaming table. Saunders dropped a thick packet marked TOP SECRET on the table in front of him. Operations orders from ComSubPac. OPERATION HIGH TIDE on its face.

Charlie glanced at Rusty and raised his eyebrows. *What were you and Saunders talking about?* Rusty frowned and shook his head as if to say: *Don't ask.*

"Gentlemen, welcome," Cooper said. "Your mission is a ferry ride and happens to be one of the most important of the war. You'll be putting the first American boots on Japanese soil. D-Day in the Pacific."

The men grinned at this news. The squadron commander pulled down a giant map of the Pacific Theater over the wall.

He tapped a collection of islands with a pointer. "In one month, we're invading Saipan. Operation TEARAWAY. At the same time, we'll take Tinian next door."

Saipan was an island in the Marianas, a crescent of volcanic islands along the edge of the Philippine Sea. About 135 miles northeast of Guam, which the United

States had won in the Spanish-American War of 1898 and was now occupied by the Japanese Empire. After the Great War, Japan gained control of the northern Marianas, Marshalls, and Carolines, formerly German colonies.

Before the current war, these islands threatened the United States. Once fortified, they could be used to cut off access to America's Western Pacific interests, namely the Philippines, Guam, and Chinese trade. In American hands, however, they provided a strategic base of operations. Air bases for bomber planes able to reach the Philippines, Taiwan, and Japan itself.

Electrified by the news, Charlie sat up straight in his chair. While the tide had turned against the Japanese Empire, victory still felt abstract. Cooper's simple statement made it real for the first time.

Two and a half years of desperate fighting had led to this. After so long, the veterans knew how to kill Japanese soldiers, sink Japanese ships. But they were tired. They were all tired. Worn to the nub.

Maybe Rusty was right. This was the beginning of the end.

"The submarines have done a hell of a job isolating Japanese bases from resupply," Cooper said. "Air attacks have reduced them. The strategy is to bypass the strongpoints and capture islands we can use as bases. Island hopping, leapfrogging, call it what you want."

Island hopping allowed the Americans to gain the

most ground with the least time and resources. It also offered the advantage of surprise because the Japanese never knew where the Americans would strike next.

The strategy was working. Since Operation CARTWHEEL began late last year, Admiral Nimitz captured Makin and Tarawa in the Gilberts then the Marshalls. Allied planes destroyed Truk naval base and began to bomb the Marianas. This had set the stage for the invasion of these islands.

"Good thing MacArthur invented this brilliant strategy," Rusty said, which prompted groans from the Navy men and a smirk from Cotten, who served under the general. Despite MacArthur's claims, the strategy originated in the Navy, largely based on war plans drafted in 1911.

"Dugout Doug will continue to isolate Rabaul and advance toward the Philippines," Cooper said. "He's made a lot of progress in the Solomons and Papua New Guinea. He was also kind enough to lend the Scouts, so let's play nice."

Rusty smiled. "My apologies to the Army."

"So where do we fit in, Coop?" Saunders asked.

The squadron commander pulled down a second map, which revealed Saipan. Eighty-five square miles. The second largest island in the Marianas after Guam.

He tapped a stretch of green on the island's western side. "Mount Fina Susu. We believe a big coastal defense gun is here overlooking the western lagoon. A very big gun, the biggest they have. So big, they gave it a name. The *Ryūsei*, Jap for 'meteor.' Only twenty-eight of them built. Twenty-seven were mounted on the Three Kings, their *Yamato*-class battleships. The last stayed in storage as a replacement until some Jap had the bright idea to use it for coastal defense."

A Type 94 naval gun, 46-centimeter bore, seventy feet long, 150 tons. It fired massive shells up to sixteen miles at 2,600 feet per second. A devastating weapon.

"Why can't we just bomb it from the air?" Saunders wondered.

"The Japs put it in a bunker," Cooper explained. "The only way to destroy it is demolitions, which is where the Scouts come in. Captain, you'll insert Cotten's team on the island. They'll proceed to Fina Susu, blow the gun, and return for extraction."

"IJN presence?"

"We don't know. Could get crowded once the invasion starts. We think that, once the Mobile Fleet gets wind we're coming, it could be their *kantai kessen*."

Charlie perked up again. *Kantai kessen*. The final showdown. The decisive battle in which the IJN would try to destroy the American fleet.

"In other words, once the shooting starts, the Japs might throw their whole navy at us," Saunders said.

"At which time, you can take a crack at any target that looks good to you. Just make sure it isn't an American ship. And speaking of which, you know well enough to stay out of their way."

"Just wanted to know if we'd get a chance to take the gloves off."

Charlie smiled. He was beginning to like Saunders.

"The primary objective is delivering and extracting the Alamo team," Cooper said. "That is top priority. If we destroy *Ryūsei*, we take the island with far fewer casualties. We take the island, and we break the Jap Empire's inner defensive ring. We'll be in striking distance of Taiwan, which will allow us to isolate the home islands. And we'll have B-29 Superfortresses within striking distance of Tokyo."

CHAPTER EIGHT
SANDTIGER'S RETURN

Sandtiger bustled with activity. A train of sailors hauled boxes of food up the gangplank to be placed in every nook and cranny of the submarine. Trucks pumped fresh water and fuel into her tanks through long thick hoses. A massive torpedo dangled from a crane as it lowered into the forward weapons hatch.

Smokey raced from one group to the next taking inventory with his clipboard. Red-faced, Spike shouted at the greenhorns, whom he loudly claimed hadn't learned anything at Submarine School.

From the bridge, Charlie and Rusty observed the crew's progress with the loadout, which was proceeding slowly. Nixon was below, ensuring all provisions were stowed properly. No sign of the captain yet.

As for Percy, he marched up the gangplank with his sea bag and saluted. "Reporting for duty, Exec."

Rusty smiled. "Welcome aboard."

No Aloha shirt today. Showered, shaved and wearing freshly laundered khakis, the young officer offered an insolent smirk.

"Rusty's taking over communications," Charlie growled. "You're taking over Jack's spot as our new torpedo officer. See to it."

"Aye, aye."

"Did you have fun?"

Percy grinned. "I have been stewed, screwed and tattooed!"

"When I'm done with you, you will regret you did."

If he wanted, he could have had Percy court-martialed and reduced to the rating of Seaman, Second Class. Or worse.

"No regrets here, Exec. If I buy the farm this time out, I won't die wishing I'd done more trim calculations. I'll wish I'd gotten more trim."

Rusty laughed as Percy went below to stow his bag. "You know, you could learn a thing or two from him," he said to Charlie.

"I'm glad you think it's funny. Half the crew don't have their dolphins, and the other half have gone soft."

The *Sandtiger*, on the other hand, was ready for war. Displacing 1,500 tons, she lay 311 feet long and twenty-seven feet wide at the beam. The Navy yard at Mare Island had given her a new streamlined superstructure to reduce her profile. Decks painted black, vertical surfaces gray. Five-inch deck gun. Six forward tubes, four aft, with a complement of twenty-four torpedoes.

Charlie couldn't wait to take her out. He gazed past the boat at the busy harbor beyond. Already, the submarine seemed crowded and boxed in, much bigger than she was. He itched to get to sea and become a speck in a vast ocean. Out there, you could both find and lose yourself.

A dungareed gorilla trudged past hauling a box of frozen vegetables on his shoulder. He stopped and winked up at Charlie.

"Good to see you again, Braddock," Rusty said.

"He got you too," the machinist said. "I thought he just had it in for me."

"Oh, I volunteered."

"You're wasted on a repair crew," Charlie said. "We need you."

"Well, ain't that touching."

"I didn't say 'want.'"

The big sailor grinned and patted the box, reminding them he had a job to do. "I'll be seeing you. Sir."

"He seems happy enough with his new posting," Rusty said after he'd left.

Charlie sighed. "When Braddock winks at you, he's promising to make your life as difficult as possible for the duration."

"Hey, you asked for him," Rusty said. "Big favor."

"I'm going to recommend he get a medal."

His friend laughed again. "God, I missed this part of the service. Why?"

"Because he keeps saving my ass every time I'm on a boat with him, but he's never gotten any credit for it. A guy who turns a wrench at just the right time is a hero. Isn't that what you told me on the 55?"

"Hey, I do sound smart sometimes. I also told you most heroes are still assholes. Ponder that deeper wisdom."

Charlie sighed again and turned away. He didn't want to talk about Braddock. He watched a twenty-foot-long torpedo lower into the weapons hatch. The new Mark 18, weighing 3,000 pounds and carrying 575 pounds of Torpex.

Wakeless, it was able to swim up to 4,000 yards without a telltale line of bubbles leading back to the submarine. It used a contact instead of a magnetic exploder, eliminating premature detonations. And it swam at the depth you wanted.

The Mark 14's problems had been solved. Still, the Mark 18 wasn't perfect. It swam slower than the Mark 14. It required a lot of maintenance, including regularly taking it out of its tube for battery recharging. The fish had a tendency to fishtail and, like the Mark 14, had no mechanism to prevent circular runs. Theoretically, a submarine skipper could fire one and sink himself.

Without Liebold, if *Sandtiger*'s crew suffered torpedo problems on this patrol, they'd have to either live with it or figure it out for themselves.

"Here come the Alamo Scouts," Rusty said.

Led by Lt. Cotten, the squad of six soldiers hauled duffel bags heavy with gear across the gangplank. They carried themselves onto the submarine as if they owned it, ignoring the protocol of asking permission to board.

"I tried to find out about them," Charlie said. "All anybody would tell me is they're an ad-hoc unit. Lots of missions in New Guinea. Killed a lot of Japs."

"I heard they know ten ways to kill you with their bare hands. The training they get is unbelievable. Nothing like the average grunt gets. Some of them are American Indians. See that big fella with the black hair? He's Cherokee. His name is Walsh, but his Cherokee name is Ahuli."

Charlie wondered what they'd done and seen during the war.

Cotten caught sight of Charlie and waved. "Where you want us?"

"Out of the way," he answered. "We'll get you boarded after loadout. Some of you will bunk with the chiefs, the rest will be quartered in the forward torpedo room. Lt. Percy will see to it."

"Aye, aye," the Scout said pointedly, as if speaking a foreign language.

The crew loaded the final provisions. The truck crews disconnected the hoses. Charlie ordered shore power and phone cabling disconnected. The Scouts went below. Sailors ran up *Sandtiger*'s battle flag—covered in meatball patches bragging of ships sunk—along the clothesline between the bow and periscope supports. After that, the Jolly Roger.

He checked his watch: 1415. The chiefs had pulled

off a miracle. They might be able to take the boat out on time. All they needed was their captain.

A jeep bounced along the pier and came to a stop among the usual crowd of tender sailors and well-wishers. Captain Saunders and Captain Squadron Commander Cooper climbed out as the Navy band struck up, "The Stars and Stripes Forever."

The officers exchanged a few words and shook hands. Looking lost, Saunders crossed the gangplank. For the first time, Charlie noticed the man had a limp.

Rusty shook his head. "He's forty pounds heavier than his last patrol."

"He was on his back for months. The war gave him a huge bill, and he paid it in full. I admire him. Not all heroes are assholes."

"You're right. I just hope he doesn't cost us anything."

"If you know something you're not telling, spit it out."

"All right," said Rusty. "Just before the briefing, he asked to have you and the other officers replaced. He wanted to pick his own men."

Charlie's stomach dropped. "I see."

"Cooper wouldn't allow it, of course. At the next meeting, Saunders was singing your praises and saying how glad he was to have you."

One more mission. After that, he would take command. He just had to tough it out. Do his duty and make it back in one piece.

He descended to the main deck and saluted. "Welcome

aboard, Captain. The loadout is complete. All hands present."

Fifty-four enlisted men, five officers.

"Very well."

"Shall I have the men muster on deck?"

Saunders' expression darkened. "Why?"

The crew had been idle for seven months. The last man they followed into combat had been killed in action. And Saunders was new to the crew.

Charlie said, "I thought the crew might appreciate a word or two from you."

"We can't afford the delay." The captain glanced at his watch. "Take us out on time, Number Two."

"Aye, aye," Charlie said and bawled, "Start the engines! Station the maneuvering watch!"

Sandtiger's big diesels roared to life, overwhelming the music played by the band, which switched to, "Anchors Aweigh."

"Stand by to single up! Take in the gangway!" He turned to Saunders. "Engines have full loading, Captain. We're ready to get underway, sir."

"Very well! Take us out. And Mr. Harrison?"

"Captain?"

"You're doing a terrific job. Keep it up."

"Thank you, sir," Charlie deadpanned. Then he glanced at Rusty, who shook his head in wonder.

The diesels pulsed. *Sandtiger* strained at her leash, snorting puffs of white smoke from her exhaust vents.

Chest purring with the vibrations, Charlie ordered the lines taken in. He was going back to sea. He put it all out of his mind—Cooper passing him over, the captain's contradictions, Percy taking off, Braddock's wink, the past. None of it mattered now. Soon, it would just be him and the big blue.

Him and the devil he'd come to know so well.

He was going to a place where a man lived in the moment.

Percy blew a whistle, and sailors lowered and removed the colors. The foghorn blasted like an angry beast. Screws churning, the submarine pivoted from the pier on stern propulsion. The crowd on the dock waved and cheered.

The legendary submarine, made famous by her captain who'd died in battle, was finally returning to the war.

CHAPTER NINE
THE MISSION

Sandtiger's diesel engines pushed her westward from Oahu. Her PT boat escort flashed signals before veering home. She was now on her own.

Below decks, Saunders laid a map and a handful of aerial recon photos on the wardroom table. "Saipan."

Charlie, Rusty, Percy, and Cotten crowded the small table for a look. Eighty-five square miles packed with Japanese troops. The recon photos showed towns, jungles, and checkerboard patterns of sugarcane fields. Fifty-four miles of coastline, most of it cliffs. Fourteen miles of beaches.

"We have a simple job to do," the captain said. "Drop the Scouts on Saipan and then extract them."

Green from hangover, Percy grinned at the prospect of a relatively safe patrol. A simple taxi ride. "Sounds easy, Captain."

"Easy, Mr. Percy? Saipan's a fortress. And we'll be sitting ducks in its shadow while we offload the commandos. Nothing easy about it."

"Yes, sir."

"After that, Fifth Fleet will enter our AO for the invasion, which may draw in the Jap Mobile Fleet for Armageddon! We'll be right in the thick of it."

Percy turned even greener. Rusty nodded with satisfaction. Charlie's pulse quickened as he pictured the great fleets roaring on the open sea. The skies booming with dogfights. And *Sandtiger* in action.

He hoped to take a crack at a battleship. He pictured the *Yamato* flying under his crosshairs. The Imperial Navy's biggest battleship, the king of the sea, 70,000 tons, bristling with guns—

Rusty nudged him and tilted his head toward the map. Charlie wiped the foolish grin off his face and paid attention.

"Mr. Grady, this is your and MacArthur's baby," Saunders said. "I'll let you take over from here."

"Thank you, Captain," said Rusty. "Aerial recon tells us the main Jap strength is up here in the northern half of the island. Fifth Fleet will feint by launching landing craft there. Meanwhile, two Marine divisions will land along the west-side beaches in the south between Mutcho Point and Agingan Point."

"How many Japs are on the island?" Percy said.

Rusty and Cotten exchanged a glance.

"Intelligence estimates maybe 15,000," Rusty said.

"Damn," Percy said, no doubt glad he'd joined the Navy. Once joined, the battle would be a bloodbath.

"Most of them will be concentrated near the beach," Cotten said. "That's how the Japs operate. They put everything on the front line with little in reserve."

Rusty pointed. "The Scouts' mission is to destroy a big coastal defense gun here at the top of Mount Fina Susu. It could play hell with the landings. To take it out, the Scouts have to land somewhere undetected. The western side of the island, where most of the beaches are, is a no-go. Heavily defended. These shoals on the western side of the island also make navigation tricky."

Charlie studied the map. He couldn't see a solution. "Then where?"

Rusty tapped the map with his finger. Magicienne Bay on the eastern side of the island. Cotten's team would go ashore between Tsutsurran and Aslito Airfield while it received a pounding by American bombers.

"That's all cliffs there," Percy said.

"Exactly. The Japs won't be watching the cliffs."

"The Scouts are supposed to climb?"

Cotten shrugged. "It's what we do."

Rusty said, "The big gun on Fina Susu is the objective. As an extra incentive for climbing it, the words apparently mean 'big boob' in Chamorro. You'll be the first Americans to conquer that sucker."

The men grinned. Charlie shot the Alamo Scout a wondering glance. Cotten and his men were like warriors from myth. Modern-day Spartans with rifles instead of spears. The six-man team would scale the cliffs, sneak across an island thick with Japanese infantry, and assault a fortified coastal gun. Then return.

From the way Cotten acted, they'd done this sort of thing before.

"I'm just glad you're on our side," Percy said.

"We drop Cotten's people June tenth and extract them June twelfth," Rusty said. "Spruance's Fifth Fleet starts shelling on the thirteenth, and then it's D-Day. Our boys take the island, we start bombing Tokyo, and the war might be over by Christmas."

The men stirred. Again, that atmosphere of excitement. History in the making. The tide had turned in this vast conflict, which at times back in '42 seemed unwinnable. The war won, they could all finally go home.

"But first, *kantai kessen*," said the captain. "The final battle. If the Japs come, it'll be one hell of a show. And we'll be right there in the middle of it."

If the Japanese committed their Mobile Fleet to battle, Fifth Fleet would be able to bring more than 100 warships to bear, including seven battleships and seven fleet carriers carrying nearly 1,000 airplanes. Charlie wondered how many warships the Japanese had at this point. They'd been reserving their strength for the final battle. While the American Navy had grown over the past two years, the IJN remained a formidable and dangerous enemy.

The war seemed winnable now, but it would be no easy feat. With the Imperial Navy still afloat, victory hung in the balance.

"Wonderful," Percy muttered.

"The Jap Navy will probably come from the west," the captain said. "My money's on the Philippines. We'll go out there and get on their tail. Kick them in the ass while Admiral Spruance bloodies their nose!"

Saunders grinned at Charlie, who smiled back. *Aye, sir. On that, we can agree.*

This patrol wouldn't just be a ferry ride. If *Sandtiger* found the Japanese Mobile Fleet, she could play an important part in what might just be the last great naval battle of the war.

Like Rusty, Charlie wanted to be there at the end.

CHAPTER TEN
ONE LITTLE THING

Sandtiger cruised at twenty knots across the vast Pacific. Along the way, the crew settled back into routines interrupted by frequent drills. Crash dive, submerged approach, battle surface, silent running, fire drills. The greenhorns got it worst of all as the chiefs laid on the firehose treatment. Charlie worked as hard as the greenhorns and took the time to learn their names. Pushed himself until he forgot his self-doubts and his cleithrophobia dulled into the background.

On the sixth day out from Pearl, he walked the submarine end to end for below-the-deck watch. He checked the valves, trim tank gauges, and bilges. Smelled for smoke, listened for dripping water, felt the air for proper ventilation.

In the engine room, he paused and closed his eyes. *Sandtiger*'s four massive Fairbanks-Morse diesel engines growled in their steel chassis. They used a remarkable opposed-piston design that doubled the number of cylinders in a relatively compact unit. The snipes labored here in sweltering heat to keep them humming.

Charlie rested his hand on a thick pipe, and the boat's vibrations flowed through him. Her urgent rhythm throbbed like love in his chest. For a moment, he joined with the submarine and reached out with his senses, taking her pulse. As with gazing at the open sea too long, you could get lost in it.

A voice close to his ear: "You all right, Exec?"

He opened his eyes. He'd been approaching some realization. Thinking about love. He wasn't like Moreau and Reynolds. It wasn't hate that drove him but love. While he no longer sought the war's brutal tests, he'd grown a deep and abiding love for the submarines. When the war pressed him, he fell back on it.

Being back at sea was like being home.

"Just listening to the music, Smokey," he said.

The quartermaster nodded. "She feels good."

"She does."

Sandtiger was in fighting trim.

"Listen, that machinist's mate you brought aboard. John Braddock."

"He's difficult."

Smokey's eyebrows shot up. "You think? He's practically trying to start a mutiny against you."

"Okay, he's an asshole."

"The boys won't have any of his sounding off. At least the guys who served with you in the Japan Sea. They know who you are and what you did."

"Maybe he's not busy enough," Charlie said. "See to it."

Smokey grinned. "Always plenty of shit work, Mr. Harrison."

Charlie pictured Braddock cleaning the bilges and found himself smiling too. He shook his head. "He's a hard case, but he's good. Give him the hard stuff."

"He's an odd duck even for a snipe. The boys call him 'the doctor.' Walks around the engine room with a stethoscope, listening to the diesels' heartbeat. Anything goes wrong, even the littlest thing, he hears it. I have to give him that."

"You need something important done, go to him."

"Well, I'm sure you had a good reason for bringing him aboard." From his tone, Smokey still wasn't buying it.

"I had a reason. Whether it's good or not, we'll find out."

Braddock was insurance.

"Keep him busy, aye, aye, sir. As for the rest of the crew, well..."

"Speak your mind," Charlie said. "I'll always take advice from you."

"Usually, my motto is a bitching sailor is a happy sailor, but I think you're pushing them too hard. The newbies call you 'the drill sergeant.'"

Charlie snorted. He didn't care what the men called him. It wasn't that long ago that being called *Hara-kiri* was an insult instead of a compliment.

"We may be in action soon," he said. "We're not as

sharp as we were when we went to the Sea of Japan."

"The crew is as good as they're going to get right now. Any more drills will do more harm than good to efficiency."

Charlie considered it. He trusted the old sea dog's judgment. "All right, Smokey. I'll give the men a few days."

He left the quartermaster and wondered how Moreau would have done it. By now, the fierce captain would surely have his crew whipped into shape. He wouldn't care if the men were tired. He set a goal and went for it with everything he had. And the crew loved him for it. They'd followed him to hell because of it.

Moreau had left very big shoes to fill.

Charlie went to Saunders' stateroom and knocked on the doorframe.

"Enter," the captain said.

He pulled aside the heavy woolen curtain and entered the cabin. The Navy called it a stateroom, but really, it offered just enough space for a bunk and desk.

A backgammon board lay on the desktop, an acey-deucey game in progress. Both players started with their chips off the table and rolled dice to bring them across the opposing player's chips to win. As far as Charlie knew, the captain played solo. An endless series of games against himself.

Rubbing a nap from his eyes, Saunders sat on the edge of the bed in his skivvies. He pulled on a khaki shirt. "Mr. Harrison. What news?"

"Just letting you know I completed the below-the-deck watch, and I'm about to go off duty for chow and a few hours of rack time."

"Very well," the captain said. "How does she head?"

"Last check, we're holding steady on 267 True. Percy is topside as officer of the deck."

Charlie and Saunders had developed a solid working relationship. For the past week, the captain avoided socializing with his officers but proved cool and competent. Saunders focused on the big picture, leaving the details to his XO.

Nothing like Rusty feared. Rusty was seldom wrong, but he was wrong about the captain. Saunders struck Charlie as a man with nothing to prove to anybody but maybe something big he needed to prove to himself. He reminded Charlie of Bob Hunter, commander of the *Sabertooth*.

"Anything else?"

"I'm planning to ease up on the drills," Charlie said. "The crew is about as efficient as I can make them."

"You do what you think is best, Mr. Harrison," the captain grunted. "Remember to include yourself in that. You push yourself too hard."

"Just trying to do my duty, sir. The boat needs a lot of care right now."

"Makes a man wonder about your demons."

Charlie frowned. "Captain?"

"I like to know who I'm sailing with and what drives them."

"I don't have any demons, sir."

"No regrets?"

He thought of Evie. Jane. "A few."

"All great men do. Every man makes mistakes. The more he tries to accomplish, the more he makes. Too many mistakes weigh a man down."

"I understand," Charlie said.

The captain still brooded over the loss of the *Flagfin*. The scuttlebutt was he'd surfaced in daylight to make an end-around on a convoy, exposing his boat to air attack. He'd then taken on responsibility for everything that followed, including the boat sinking in the Yellow Sea under another captain's command.

Charlie found it troubling. Battle debris blocking a valve. A single mistake in the rush of combat. One little thing could sink a ship or a man.

"We can't change the past," the captain said. "But we can repeat it. Put ourselves to the same test. That's how you change the outcome. Rewrite your history. Make it right."

Howard Saunders wanted one more chance at bat. One more shot at a homerun to erase his devastating strikeout. Charlie had to give him credit. Like everybody else, the man was tired. The war had taken something from him, but he kept fighting. He didn't give up.

The captain added, "Are you trying to correct a mistake?"

"It's the future mistakes I worry about, sir."

"You're a lucky man. This boat and its bachelor officers. I envy you young hotshots. Your biggest potential and mistakes lay ahead of you."

"I've made plenty of mistakes, sir. I just try to look forward, that's all."

"Right." Saunders waved his paw to dismiss him. "That's enough philosophy before breakfast, Mr. Harrison. I won't hold you up from your leisure."

"Thank you, sir." On his way out, Charlie pointed to the backgammon game. "I hope you win."

CHAPTER ELEVEN
THE SHIP

On the bridge, Charlie and Smokey braced against the boat's roll. They aimed their binoculars into the sprawling darkness ahead of the bow. Perched on the shears, the lookouts scanned their sectors. On a cloudy night like this, the black ocean stretched into infinity all around them.

Soon, they'd make landfall. Saipan.

And once they did, *Sandtiger* would dive for the final approach into Magicienne Bay. She was ideal for this kind of mission, one requiring stealth.

This time, Charlie was determined to spot the landmass before the quartermaster, who had the best night vision among any man he knew.

Lightning flecked the northern horizon.

"Contact," Smokey said.

Charlie shook his head. Bested again. "I wish I had your night vision. I can't believe you can see Saipan from here."

"I can't. I spotted a ship. Relative bearing one-two-oh

off the starboard quarter." The man pointed. "Saw him right there in a lightning flash."

Charlie trained his glasses on the stretch of sea to the northeast. He was about to give up when he spotted it. A tiny black smudge on the horizon.

"That's what, 15,000 yards?"

"More like twenty, and he's closing," Braddock said from the shears. "Try eating more carrots, sir."

"Shut your dick-hole, Braddock," Smokey growled.

Charlie ignored the machinist. "Escorts?"

"None that I could see."

"He must be coming from Wake. A warship. Maybe a supply ship."

Wake Island. On December 11, 1941, Japanese forces attempted their first invasion of the fortified atoll. Marines, Navy personnel, and civilians fought together to repel the attack. Twelve days later, carrier planes supported another assault, and Wake fell. The Japanese still occupied it.

"If he's a supply ship, he's brave coming out here by himself."

Charlie said into the bridge speaker, "Conn, Bridge."

"Bridge, Conn," Rusty said. "Go ahead, Charlie."

"Contact, bearing one-two-oh relative off the starboard quarter, about 15,000 yards and closing. Unsure of ship type."

"Received. Wait."

"Land ho," the quartermaster said.

Charlie smirked. "You're something else, Smokey. Conn, Bridge. Need to add we've just made landfall on Saipan."

"Got it," came the reply.

"Think the Old Man will go for it?" Smokey asked him. "If it's a maru, it'd be easy pickings. We veer north a bit, and we'll be in his track."

"I hear you. But there's Saipan, and we've got a schedule to keep. The commandos have a date with a Jap gun."

"Bridge, Conn," Rusty said. "We're gonna do a Sugar Jig sweep."

"Roger," Charlie said.

The upgraded SJ radar, able to detect land and sea contacts up to 30,000 yards. The mast extended. The head rotated, sweeping the sea.

Smokey said, "He's thinking about it. The target's practically coming right at us. We could swing north a bit, drill some holes in him, and be back in time—"

"Clear the topsides," the bridge speaker blared.

"Ah, well."

Charlie swished down the ladder and landed on the deck. The lookouts followed. From above, Smokey called out that the hatch was secure.

Captain Saunders said into the 1MC, "Dive, dive, dive!"

The klaxon blasted twice.

The ship had tempted the captain, but he was sticking

with the plan. Getting the Scouts onto Saipan remained top priority.

"Maneuvering, Conn," Rusty said into the 7MC. "Stop the main engines. Switch to battery power. Rig out the bow planes. Manifold, close the main induction."

The main induction—the main air intake for the engines—clanged shut.

"We've got a green board," Rusty reported after inspecting the Christmas tree's indicator lights. "All compartments report ready to dive, Captain."

"Very well, Mr. Grady," Saunders said. "Dive! Planes, sixty-five feet."

The planesmen turned the big brass wheels in opposite directions, keeping their eyes on the inclinometer.

"Manifold, open all main vents," Rusty said.

Seawater flooded the ballast tanks, making the boat heavy. Charlie braced his legs as the deck tilted fifteen degrees. The depth gauge needle slowly turned as *Sandtiger* slid into the sea.

"That Jap doesn't know how lucky he is," the captain muttered.

"Close all vents," Rusty said. "Blow negative."

High-pressure air shot into the flooded negative tank to restore buoyancy, which would allow the boat to maintain her target depth.

"Open the bulkhead flappers. Start the ventilation. We're at sixty-five feet with good trim, Captain. Speed, three knots."

Sandtiger had returned to stealth mode, hidden under the water, able to approach the island's coast without fear.

"Very well," Saunders said. "Take us to Saipan."

CHAPTER TWELVE
D-DAY

Five miles from the island, *Sandtiger* still cruised submerged. Sweating in shorts and sandals, the crew manned their stations.

In the conning tower, officers and sailors tensed as the submarine knifed toward the lion's den. Percy at the torpedo data computer aft to port, Rusty hunched over the radioman aft to starboard. Nixon near the sonar just forward of the TDC. Charlie and Captain Saunders at the plotting table by the periscopes.

"Up scope!" the captain ordered.

He leaned his bulk against the observation periscope, arm draped over the handle. Swiveled to gain a view of the island and surrounding sea.

"Steady," Saunders said.

Charlie felt a shift in the boat. Saipan's northern point extended into the north equatorial drift current, creating a southerly local current along the island's east side. The current slackened as the submarine entered Magicienne Bay.

Land now surrounded her on three sides. Once *Sandtiger* surfaced, coastal watchers would be able to see her.

"Depth under the keel?" said Saunders.

The echo sounder emitted a single ping.

"Eighty-five feet," Rusty reported.

"Keep it coming, Mr. Grady."

Rusty called out fathometer readings while the captain tweaked their course. No idle chatter. Necks clenched with tension, the crew focused on the job. Charlie hated being here as much as they did.

If spotted, an enemy ship might move in astern, boxing in the submarine in the bay's shallow waters. Or the Japanese might call in an artillery strike. A patrol plane could roar over the cliffs from the airfield just a few miles away. The Japanese might even have coastal guns guarding the bay.

Saipan was a fortress, and *Sandtiger* was sneaking right up to its back door. Nothing easy about it.

Below the submarine, the sea bottom sloped sharply. Rusty's next fathometer reading revealed just thirty-five feet below the keel. With each passing moment, *Sandtiger* came closer to running aground.

"Helm, come left to two-double-oh," Saunders ordered.

"Come left to two-double-oh, aye, Captain."

"All stop."

"All stop, aye." The helmsman selected ALL STOP on

the annunciator, which responded with a bell chime.

"Up scope!"

The captain hugged the periscope, humming a grating tune as he scanned for landmarks noted on his charts.

Sandtiger had entered Magicienne Bay. The captain knew where she was with a fair degree of precision. The dead reckoning tracer plotted latitude and longitude on a chart. However, right now, he needed to be exact.

A coral reef girded most of the coastline here. A fringing reef close to the shore. Though concealed by the high tide, the coral might still be near enough to the surface to tear an inflatable raft to shreds.

According to the charts, a small parcel of coast directly in the center of the bay shoreline had no reef. The only problem was it stretched about a mile along the coast. If the southerly current was too strong, it might push the rafts into the reefs.

As a result, the officers had to choose the launch and landing points carefully. The ideal time to launch was coming soon, when tidal and wave energy slackened. During this period, the tidal stream stilled before ebbing toward low tide.

They'd done what they could. After the launch, it was all on the Alamo Scouts, who would have to paddle quickly to cross a mile of water and reach the cliffs.

Captain Saunders grunted, apparently satisfied. "Stand by to surface. Mr. Harrison, get the Scouts ready to go topside. We'll be surfacing just high enough and long enough to get them off the boat. We're a sitting duck here."

"Aye, aye, Captain," Charlie said and hustled below deck.

The Alamo Scouts lined the passageway aft of the control room. Weapons slung over their shoulders, Lt. Cotten and three Scouts wore camouflage fatigues and utility caps. No insignia or tags. The other two, posing as sugarcane farmers, wore straw planter's hats and civilian shirts and slacks. The giant Cherokee stared back at him with his gleaming black eyes, taciturn as ever.

Charlie said, "We're about to surface the boat, Jonas. Get ready."

The lieutenant removed his semiautomatic pistol, checked the action, and returned it to his holster. Cotten had shown Charlie the fitted suppressor, a remarkable innovation. With this device, the long-barreled pistol fired with a dramatically reduced sound and muzzle flash, ideal for commando operations.

"Thanks for the heads-up," he said. "What's that you got on your face?"

"Red-tinted goggles. They help me adapt for night vision." Since their introduction, boats no longer rigged for red.

"Pretty neat," the lieutenant said. The Navy had its own impressive gadgets. "What's it like outside?"

"Cloudy. No moon. The stand of the tide. Still, it's going to be dicey."

Cotten shrugged. "It usually is."

The surfacing alarm blasted three times. The soldiers followed him up the ladder to the hatch, where Smokey waited.

Sandtiger rose on a zero bubble to break the surface with an even keel.

"Open the hatch," the captain commanded.

The quartermaster undogged it with a rubber mallet and opened it a crack. A burst of water. The boat's foul atmosphere rushed past the men and whistled out the crack. Once the pressure equalized, Smokey pushed it open.

Charlie mounted to the bridge. The bay's waters churned over the submarine's decks, which were still awash. *Sandtiger* lay at a depth that allowed only her sail to rise above the water. Ready to dunk fast. The captain wasn't taking any chances.

He swept the darkness with his binoculars. The volcanic island loomed black all around. The night air warm and wet. A land breeze carried a thick jungle smell along with a brief tang of smoke. Not from *Sandtiger*'s exhaust but fires that had burned out after American planes bombed the airfield earlier in the day.

No signs of life. The Japanese were out there, though, in their thousands. Dug in and waiting.

"All clear," he called down.

The Alamo Scouts spilled out. Carbon dioxide hissed into the inflatable, which cracked loudly as it expanded. Three minutes later, it was ready to launch.

The commandos piled their weapons and gear into the raft then climbed aboard.

Charlie lowered his binoculars. "Godspeed, Jonas. Good luck to you."

The soldiers began to paddle in deep, clean strokes.

"Remember!" Cotten called back with a grin, reciting his unit motto.

A mile to go until they reached the talus piled at the base of the cliffs.

"Think they can do it?" Smokey asked Charlie.

"Are you a praying man?"

"When the shit hits the fan, I get very personal with the almighty, Mr. Harrison."

"Then pray for those men," Charlie said. "They'll need all the help they can get."

"Bridge, Conn," Rusty said over the bridge speaker. "Clear the topsides."

Charlie slid down the ladder. Above, Smokey called out he'd secured the hatch. Already, the boat felt lighter without the Scouts. *Sandtiger* was no longer a ferry. She'd become a deadly warship again, ready for a fight.

"Dive, dive, dive!" the captain said. "Planes, sixty-five feet."

Sandtiger slid into the water on propulsion and leveled out at periscope depth.

"Up scope!"

The observation periscope slid smoothly from its well. Saunders slapped the handles down and hugged the scope. Swung it slowly until he froze.

"I've got them. Paddling like crazy. Straight up shit's creek!"

The sailors smiled at their stations. The captain swiveled the scope.

"No activity," he added. "Goddamnit, they're drifting. Cotten knows, they're correcting. Paddling hard as they can against the current. They reached the cliffs. They're anchoring to the rock. Two of them are climbing. Mr. Harrison!"

"Aye, Captain?"

"Get over here and stay on the Scouts. Let me know when they all make it to the top of the cliff."

As Charlie nestled his face against the rubber eyepiece, the captain ordered the attack periscope raised to scan for threats. *Sandtiger* circled in the bay. For the next hour, the men leaned against their scopes.

At six times magnification, Charlie saw the team clearly. Two Scouts climbed the limestone cliff, hammering anchors into the rock and pausing to rest in two small caves. The next pair ascended using the ropes. They hauled up the gear.

Then the last two made the climb with the deflated raft.

His chest tightened. He realized he hadn't been breathing. He took a deep breath and let it out nice and slow. "They made it, Captain. They're at the top."

For the first time in the war, American soldiers stepped onto Japanese soil.

"Let's get the hell out of this mousetrap," the captain said. "Down scopes! Helm, come right to one-two-oh. All ahead standard."

The helmsman steered *Sandtiger* onto the new course. The men stretched at their stations to release their tension.

"Mr. Grady!" Saunders barked.

"Aye, Captain?"

"It seems you and MacArthur might actually know what you're doing."

Rusty caught Charlie's gaze and winked. Charlie touched his knuckle to his forehead in salute.

"No more babysitting for us," Saunders added. "Not it's our turn."

Charlie: "Sir?"

The captain grinned. "Now we go get that bastard, Mr. Harrison."

CHAPTER THIRTEEN
THE CHASE

No longer a ferry, *Sandtiger* became a hunter again.

Her conning tower broke the surface. The SJ radar rose and spun on its mast.

Captain Saunders leaned against the console and peered over the radarman's shoulder to study the PPI scope. Concentric rings overlaid the glowing cathode tube screen, delineating ranges from 100 to 1,000 yards.

A green smear swept around the screen and revealed the big fuzzy landmass of Saipan. No enemy ships. The target had reached the other side of the island, where it was now undetectable by the submarine's radar.

"He hightailed it," the captain growled. "Skipped right on by while we were playing taxi. Probably safe and sound in Tanapag Harbor by now."

Charlie eyed the display. "Not necessarily, Captain."

"If you got a bright idea, I'm all ears."

"He might have steamed straight past Saipan and is now heading for the Philippines to take on cargo to bring back to the Home Islands."

Captain Sanders stomped to the plotting table and inspected the charts. He'd have to conn the *Sandtiger* around Naftan Point. Then cross the narrow stretch of water separating Saipan and Tinian. Once he cleared Agingan Point, he could order another radar sweep without Saipan blocking it.

If the target were, in fact, on his way to the Philippines, *Sandtiger* would already be on an intercept course.

Charlie glanced at the clock. Plenty of darkness left.

"We won't make it in time to intercept him," Percy said.

"Lots of time if we do it on the surface," the captain said.

"The water separating Saipan and Tinian is only a couple of miles across. This close to the shore, we'll be visible to any coastal watcher who's even half-awake. The Japs could have guns overlooking the passage."

"Even more reason to get through as fast as possible, Mr. Percy."

Rusty joined them at the plotting table. "Captain, he's right. I recommend we do our hunting in safer waters. We have to rendezvous with the Scouts in forty-eight hours. Our first responsibility is to get them out."

"I know my responsibility very well, Mr. Grady. Because I'm the goddamn captain! A captain with a short shit list and a very long memory!"

"I withdraw my comments, Skipper," Percy said, looking sick. "It's all good."

Rusty shot Charlie a look. "Yeah. Another bright idea."

Charlie shrugged. He and his friend always had a very different risk tolerance.

"Helm, plot a course that will swing us around Naftan Point and directly between Saipan and Tinian," Saunders said.

"Aye, aye, Captain," the helmsman said.

Saunders keyed the 1MC. "All compartments, rig to surface!"

The klaxon blasted three times. Charlie still had his night adaptation goggles and binoculars around his neck. He put the goggles on, tinting the world red.

"Maneuvering, stand by to switch from motors to diesels," said Rusty, who was still acting as diving officer. "Answer bells on main engines on surfacing. Secure ventilation. Shut the bulkhead flappers."

"Lookouts to the conning tower!" Charlie said.

The sailors returned to join him on the ladder, including Braddock.

The machinist's mate winked. "I hear we're gonna give the Japs some target practice, sir."

"Put a cork in it, Braddock," Charlie growled.

"All compartments report rigged to surface," the telephone talker said in the conning tower below.

"Ready to surface in every respect, Captain," Rusty said.

"Very well! Take her up."

"Control, blow all main ballast tanks. Blow negative."

High-pressure air shot into the ballast tanks, pushing the water out. The planesmen angled the boat. *Sandtiger* lunged from the sea and righted with a mighty splash, her decks draining in waterfalls.

"Depth, eighteen feet," Rusty said. "We're surfaced."

"Open the hatch!"

Smokey undogged the hatch. Charlie returned to the bridge and swept all around with his glasses. No contacts.

"All clear!" he said.

The lookouts piled out and took up their stations. The engines fired in sequence, belching smoke. *Sandtiger* raced forward, pitching as she turned into the gentle swells. Briny spray filled the humid air. To the west, Saipan's black hulk filled the horizon. Right now, the Alamo Scouts threaded through jungle and sugarcane fields toward their target, hopefully still safe.

The captain hauled himself up and joined Charlie and Smokey on the bridge. "We're having fun now, Mr. Harrison!"

"Yes, sir."

Saunders smiled while he scanned the cliffs with his binoculars. "Now let's see if your instincts are as good as everybody says."

The captain certainly appeared to be having fun. Again, Charlie wondered at Rusty's concern. From what Charlie had seen, Saunders had nerves of steel.

"That's Naftan Point," Smokey said.

"About seven miles, and we'll be through the islands." Captain Saunders laughed. "If we live that long!"

Sandtiger knifed between Saipan and Tinian on all

four mains. Again, a whiff of smoke. Fires burned out after American airstrikes.

Charlie kept his binoculars trained on Tinian to the southwest. "I'm actually surprised we haven't been spotted yet."

"We have, Mr. Harrison! They just don't have any big guns here, and by the time the Japs get an artillery battery out of bed and shooting, we'll be long gone." The captain lowered his binoculars to shout into the bridge speaker, "Conn, Bridge. Warm up the Sugar Jig. Stand by to make an automatic sweep on the PPI."

"Aye, aye, Captain," came the reply.

"On the other hand, Mr. Harrison, if there are any warships in the area, we can expect to have company very soon."

"Let's hope not," Charlie said, though a part of him found the idea of tangling with a destroyer intriguing. The captain's enthusiasm was infectious, making him feel invincible even though he knew he was far from immortal.

The submarine cleared the islands, and the Pacific opened up.

"Conn, Bridge," Saunders said. "Let's have that sweep on the Sugar Jig."

Overhead, the SJ radar spun into action.

"Bridge, Conn. Contact, bearing two-one-oh. Angle on the bow, starboard fifty. Speed, twelve knots. Range, 20,000 yards."

"Very well!" The captain rubbed his meaty paws together. "Very well, indeed. We got him. Battle stations, torpedo!"

Below decks, the general alarm gonged throughout the boat. Bearded sailors rushed to stations on sandaled feet.

"Bridge, Conn. All compartments report battle stations manned."

"Conn, Bridge. Have Mr. Percy start a plotting party. Mr. Nixon will recommend a normal approach."

"Wait, Bridge."

"Yup," said the captain.

"Nixon says steer three-five-five," Rusty said over the bridge speaker.

"Yup. And?"

"And that's it, Captain. It's a textbook approach. We'll run right into him. We can shoot with a starboard thirty angle on the bow at a thousand yards."

"Music to my ears! How long?"

"Ten minutes."

"Raise the scope and see if you can tell me what we'll be shooting. I need eyes on him. Helm, steer three-five-five!"

Rusty acknowledged the order. *Sandtiger* shifted slightly left on her heading. The observation periscope rose from its well.

"Actually, I've got him," Smokey said. "A single-stack freighter."

"Bridge, Conn. We've identified the target as the *Myūru Maru*, a cargo vessel, 430 feet long, 6,900 tons, draft 25 feet."

A flash of light.

Charlie yelled, "Contact!"

They all saw it now. A ship approached from Tanapag Harbor in the north, running lights blazing. A powerful searchlight swept the water.

"That would be a warship," Charlie said. "Looking for us is my guess."

"The plan's the same," Captain Saunders said. "Conn, Bridge. We've got company on the way. We'll submerge at 2,000 yards. Advise on approach."

"Recommend steer three-five-oh," Rusty said.

"Do it. We'll dive at 2,300 yards."

Charlie kept his binoculars zeroed on the distant beam of light. So far, the warship hadn't spotted the *Sandtiger*. It steamed down the coast, zigzagging and sweeping the sea with its light.

Then it darted onto a westward heading.

"He's changing course!" Charlie cried.

The captain raised his binoculars to look for himself. "Has he seen us?"

"He's heading for the freighter."

The Japanese ship knew an American submarine operated in the area but didn't know where. So he took the most practical course. Protect the nearest friendly ship.

Rusty: "Bridge, Conn. Target is at 2,300 yards."

"Clear the topsides," Captain Saunders barked. "Stand by to dive. That Jap skipper will get here just in time to see the show."

CHAPTER FOURTEEN
RUNNING HOT

Sandtiger slid into the sea, holding steady on a course that brought her ever closer to her prey.

"Range, 1,800 yards," the soundman reported. "Target is on the same bearing. Angle on the bow starboard forty and closing."

"Where's the warship, Captain?" Charlie asked.

"Don't worry about him, Mr. Harrison! Sound, stay on the freighter."

Percy fed the information into the TDC.

"Forward Torpedo, make ready the tubes," Saunders added. "Order of tubes is one, two, three, and four. High speed. Target is the freighter."

"Depth, Captain?" Percy said.

"Twenty feet."

A dull thud vibrated in the hull as the outer torpedo doors opened. Water flooded the tubes. The torpedo compartment reported the tubes were armed and ready to fire.

"Range, 1,300 yards," the soundman said. "Same

bearing. Angle on the bow, starboard thirty-three and closing."

"He has no idea," Rusty said, shaking his head.

"Target is slowing," the soundman called out. "Eight knots."

"He's starting to figure it out," Captain Saunders said. "He sees the warship coming after him. He'll turn soon. Nixon!"

At the plotting table, the engineering officer jumped. "What?"

"Give me a goddamn course correction!"

"Steer three-five-six."

"Helm, steer three-five-six! Up scope!"

Their textbook approach was quickly becoming complicated as real-world variables popped up one after the other.

"Warship is pinging," the soundman reported. "Long-range sonar."

The captain hugged the scope, humming his grating tune. "There you are, you good-looking bastard. We're gonna get a shot off by the skin of our teeth. He's coming on! Stand by, Forward! Final bearing, mark!"

Charlie called out his reading from the bearing ring on the other side of the periscope shaft. "Two-one-oh!"

"Range, mark!"

"A thousand yards!"

Percy twisted the knobs on the TDC. "Set! Shoot anytime, Skipper!"

"FIRE ONE!"

Rusty pressed the firing plunger. "On the way!"

After eight seconds: "Fire two!" Then, "Fire three! Fire four!"

Sandtiger bucked as she unleashed her shots into the sea.

"Stay on those fish, Sound," the captain said, his face still pressed against the scope's eyepiece.

"Three of our fish are running hot, straight, and normal," the soundman said. "The second torpedo's out of action, sir. I can't get a fix on it."

"How long?"

Rusty looked up from his stopwatch. "Thirty seconds."

The captain continued to keep the periscope raised.

"Captain! Where's the warship?" Charlie said.

"I said don't worry about—"

Thunder drowned out his last words. The explosions rocked *Sandtiger*.

"Three hits!" the captain yelled. "The first right under his stack, the second abaft of the stack, the third clipped his stern! He's going down in pieces!"

The eerie sound of scraping metal filled the sea as the *Myūru Maru* plummeted to the bottom of the Pacific.

And over it, the piercing pings of echo ranging.

"Down scope! Pull the plug! Take her down, emergency!"

Charlie grabbed a length of overhead piping as the boat tilted downward, delivering the submarine and her crew back to the depths.

The crew had performed flawlessly. All the drills had paid off.

Saunders said, "Give me a bearing, Sound."

"One-seven-five," the soundman said. "Light screws, range 3,000 yards, thirty knots. Sounds like a destroyer. He's heading to where the freighter sank. One-seven-four-and-a-half, one-seven-four—"

"Helm, come left to two-double-oh," said the captain.

Standard operating procedure, keeping his stern facing the target. So far, so good, Charlie thought. They'd bagged their freighter and were making a clean getaway. The enemy destroyer didn't have a fix on their location.

They might get out of this without a single depth charge dropped.

The telephone talker blanched at his station. "Captain! Forward Torpedo says one of our fish is jammed in the number two tube. It's running hot."

Charlie moved to the telephone talker's station and grabbed the 7MC headset. "This is the exec." Voices from different compartments shouted in his ear. "Clear the line! Forward, give me a damage report."

He got the story straight from the chief. The torpedo had started to fishtail as it left the tube, jamming itself partway out. As a result, they couldn't secure the outer tube door. Soon, the torpedo's propulsion would fail, leaving it unable to move on its own. Worse, the torpedo's arming element was outside the submarine and had likely armed itself in the time since the shot fired.

At any moment, the torpedo might explode and take the bow with it.

Charlie threw the headset down. "Captain, I'm going forward."

"Report when you get there, Number Two."

"Aye, aye. Nixon, I'll need you with me."

Pale faced, the engineering officer nodded meekly and followed. They slid down the ladder to the control room and hunched to pass through the compartment's watertight door.

"Right behind you, Mr. Harrison," Smokey said.

Charlie was glad to have him along. He bent again to enter the smoky torpedo room. Manned by six sailors who also bunked there, Forward Torpedo was the largest compartment in the submarine. Twelve massive stacked torpedoes crowded the room. Empty skids marked the fish fired at the freighter. Pipes, valves, and gauges filled most of the rest of the space.

In combat, Chief Petty Officer Randall oversaw operations. Two sailors manned the tubes and manifold. Another checked the angle set on each torpedo's gyroscope, and another worked a manual firing key in case the torpedo didn't respond to the electrical firing command from Control. The remaining two sailors served as the reload crew, delivering fresh torpedoes using a chain hoist.

Chief Randall ran a good shop here. The torpedomen worked together like a well-oiled machine. Charlie never saw anything out of place during his inspections, not even a piece of litter on the deck.

Rusty said over the 1MC, *"All compartments, rig for collision."*

Smoke from the jammed torpedo's burning engine permeated the air. A pencil-thin wisp of smoke streamed from the number three tube's closed vent. Then it abruptly stopped. The torpedo's engine had burned out.

"Chief, get your people out of here and dog the door," Charlie said. "We've got to figure this out."

"Aye, aye, Mr. Harrison," Randall said. "You heard the exec! Move your asses aft!"

The sailors hustled from the room. The heavy watertight door slammed and locked. The steady pinging quickened and intensified. The destroyer had switched to short scale, its skipper confident he was closing on his quarry.

"Any ideas, Chief?" Charlie asked him.

"We can't close the outer door," Randall said. "We can't open the tube door to pull it back in, or the compartment will flood. And if that tin can up there starts dropping depth charges, it'll go off and blow us to hell!"

"Even if the tin can doesn't," Smokey said. "We hit a patch of rough water, and sooner or later our goose is cooked."

Charlie stared at the men as the horror sank in. They might already be dead and simply not know it yet.

He swallowed and said, "Any ideas on how to get out of this?"

Randall and Smokey glanced at each other. Neither said a word.

"Nixon?"

The engineering officer was shaking. "This is bad. Really bad."

"Hey." Charlie grabbed the skinny officer's shoulders. "Look at me, Nixon. We're going to be all right, but we need to figure this out. Any ideas?"

The man's glazed eyes flickered. "Only one way out."

"What is it?"

"We shoot it out with a blast of high-pressure air while we reverse. Then we pray it doesn't explode until we get far enough away from it."

CHAPTER FIFTEEN
NO CHOICE

They stared at Nixon in disbelief.

"Jesus," Randall said. "With all due respect, Mr. Nixon, you're off your nut."

"You got a better idea?" Smokey said.

The stocky chief opened his mouth then closed it. Shook his head.

"Then we have no choice," Charlie said.

The men gazed up as the Japanese destroyer's screws thrashed the water overhead. Loud pinging filled the room, grating their already raw nerves.

"*Rig for silent running*," Rusty said over the 1MC.

The boat had reached a depth of 400 feet.

He keyed the 7MC. "Conn, Forward Torpedo."

Rusty answered. "Go, Charlie."

He explained the problem and its only solution, keeping his voice as low as possible. The destroyer's constant, ghostly pinging reverberated throughout the hull.

"You're kidding," Rusty said.

"Let me talk to the captain."

"Wait."

"Hurry!" Charlie hissed, but Rusty was gone. "Chief, how many men will we need to shoot out the torpedo?"

"Just one," the man said sulkily. "I suppose that's me."

"We'll also need to secure the outer door afterwards. We'll need three men altogether."

Whoosh whoosh whoosh whoosh

PING-PING

Randall flinched. "He's got us."

"He'll drop depth charges on his next run," Smokey said.

Charlie punched the 7MC. "Conn, we need an answer!"

"Wait," Rusty said.

"We can't wait," he exploded. No answer. "What the hell!"

"Oh God," Nixon said. "This is not good. I don't want to be here, please."

"If the bow blows off, the boat's going down," Smokey told him. "Me, I'd rather die in a flash than slowly, gasping for air in the dark."

"Oh God," Nixon said.

Charlie gripped the man's shoulders again. "Nixon, I want you to go aft and bring back helmets and flak jackets. Can you do that?"

The engineering officer swallowed and nodded. "Aye, aye."

They undogged the door. Gawking torpedomen

crowded the next compartment. Nixon barreled into them.

"Make a hole for him!" Charlie said. "And hurry up!"

The thrashing overhead grew louder. The destroyer was making his run.

Whoosh whoosh whoosh whoosh

Charlie grabbed a handhold. Sweat poured into his eyes. He clenched them shut as he struggled to control his breathing.

Ker-choon! Ker-choon!

Splashes.

Charlie's eyes flashed open.

WHAM! WHAM! WHAM!

Water hammer punched the thick steel hull and shook the submarine. Light bulbs popped, plunging the compartment into near darkness. Cork insulation splintered along the bulkhead and filled the air with swirling shards and dust.

By some miracle, the torpedo didn't explode.

WHAM! WHAM! WHAM! WHAM!

The boat heeled over with an alarming list. Slick with sweat, Charlie's grip failed, and he crashed to the deck. Randall fell and tumbled against a torpedo skid. Smokey held on, roaring as the boat managed to right itself.

Again, the torpedo held and didn't blow them all into the sea.

The thrashing faded as the destroyer completed its run.

Soon, it would be back.

Smokey helped Charlie to his feet. "Time to start praying, sir. You all right?"

He responded with a weak nod, hands on his knees and coughing on the dust. Randall sat on the deck moaning, his fingers probing a deep cut along his scalp that poured blood. Smokey pulled off his skivvy shirt, balled it up, and pressed it against the wound as Charlie staggered to the 7MC.

"Conn, Forward Torpedo!"

Rusty's voice: "Charlie? Charlie!"

"We need to get this hot fish out now. Our luck can't keep holding."

"The captain's not responding."

"What?"

"He's sitting with his back against the TDC."

Charlie's breath caught. "He's wounded?"

"No," Rusty said. "His mouth keeps moving, but he's not really saying anything. I think he's praying. We're not even taking evasive action."

"Order all back full. Make your trim as good as you can. After we build up enough speed, we'll shoot the bad fish out with high-pressure air."

"You want me to take the conn?"

"You're going to have to."

A pause, then: "That's mutiny."

The compartment door opened. Nixon and two sailors handed big steel helmets and flak jackets to Smokey.

Charlie put his back to them. "No choice, Rusty. This is our only chance."

The heavy steel door closed behind him.

Another pause. "All right."

Charlie turned. "Get ready—"

Braddock handed him his helmet and flak jacket. "Here we go again, sir."

Charlie cinched the strap on his bulky steel helmet with trembling hands. Rusty was as good as his word. The compartment shook as the boat's momentum reversed. Maneuvering had switched from standard to all back full.

"The chief's had it," Smokey said. "Braddock volunteered to take his place."

"Good man," Charlie said.

"I'd rather die quick than suffocate slow," the sailor said.

"That's just what I said," Smokey said. "We need to build up the air pressure feeding the tube as high as it'll go."

"I can do that," Braddock said and went to the manifold.

Sandtiger lurched faster as the Japanese destroyer closed in for another run.

"Come on," Charlie growled at the engines, willing them to work harder to bring the boat to full speed.

Braddock finished building up the air pressure and sat on the deck. He grabbed hold of the empty skid. "Better hold on, sir."

Rusty said over the 7MC: *"We're at full speed astern."*

Whoosh whoosh whoosh

Smokey's hand hovered over the firing key. His eyes met Charlie's.

Charlie gritted his teeth against the surge of bile rising from his stomach. "Do it, and God help us."

The quartermaster punched the firing key and wrapped his hands around the nearest piping. Charlie grabbed a handhold as well, bracing himself for one hell of a shock.

Sandtiger bucked as a thousand pounds of air pressure slammed into the dead torpedo and hurled it from the tube.

Overhead, the enemy destroyer closed in.

WHOOSH WHOOSH WHOOSH

One, Charlie thought. *Two.* He didn't want to count anymore, but he forced himself to concentrate. *And three. And four, four, four—*

BOOM

The shockwave smashed *Sandtiger*'s bow. The deck plates buckled. The remaining light bulbs shattered. Charlie's vision went searing white, and for a moment, he became bodiless. Heaven, he thought, was beautiful, made entirely of light.

He was flying, tumbling through space.

And came to in several inches of cold seawater.

The white light was gone, nothing more than an afterimage superimposed over black and gray. His vision blurry and stinging. He blinked to clear water from his eyes. The room came into focus. The torpedo compartment lit by emergency lights.

Water shot across the room from cracks in the number two tube door.

Braddock was already on his feet and working the crank to secure the outer door manually. Charlie tried to stand but fell to his hands and knees. The deck remained tilted as *Sandtiger* drifted with a pronounced up angle.

He made it to his feet and clambered up the incline, dodging jets of water powerful enough to hurl him back to the other end of the compartment. Smokey sprawled groaning on an empty torpedo skid.

And the water continued to rise.

"Give me a hand," Braddock said. "Somehow the bow held, but I ain't gonna fucking drown in here!"

Charlie made it up the incline, gripped the crank, and pulled as hard as he could. Slowly, it turned. The two men grunted at the strain.

The water pressure faded with each turn. The outer door had escaped damage and was closing.

"Almost got it," Braddock gasped.

The leaks went slack and sputtered out, leaving them exhausted and dripping in the misty air.

Rusty's voice from the 7MC: *"Charlie? Charlie? Answer me!"*

Charlie limped to the speaker and picked up the handset. "We secured the torpedo door, but we've got smaller leaks. Send a repair party on the double. And send the pharmacist's mate. Smokey's hurt."

"You got it, brother," Rusty said. "Hang tight."

He slumped to the deck next to Braddock and rested his back against the bulkhead. "I don't hear screws."

"Or depth charges going off," the machinist said. "The Jap thinks he sank us."

"We got very lucky."

"No kidding. What does it take to kill you, sir? You got the luck of the Irish."

"You did good," Charlie said. "Now you know why I brought you."

The compartment door swung open. Sailors splashed inside.

Braddock glared back at him. "Maybe you're starting to figure out why I didn't want to come along."

CHAPTER SIXTEEN
ROCKS AND SHOALS

A shot of medicinal brandy warming his chest, Charlie peeled off his uniform and collapsed on his rack. Every part of him ached. Rusty trudged in and sighed as he climbed into the overhead bunk. Percy had taken over as officer of the deck.

They lay in silence, unable to sleep. Still processing what had happened.

"How's the captain?" Charlie asked.

The overhead mattress rustled. "He went to his cabin and hasn't come out."

"You were right. About him."

"He's a good man pushed too far," Rusty said.

Charlie had seen many good men crack in combat. Men screaming, crying, pissing themselves, losing all reason.

Being depth-charged was a long, bumpy ride along the edge of death by instant drowning or slow asphyxiation. Ships thrashing like trains overhead. The constant pinging that sped up as the enemy closed in.

The strings of explosions that battered the helpless boat and its sailors, rattling them like peanuts in a can.

And being depth-charged with a hot torpedo in one of the tubes—well, he'd never experienced terror like that before. Every second of survival a dice roll. He still had the shakes from it.

"Do you think," Charlie said, "what happened to him could happen to us?"

"Everybody has a breaking point. Constant pressure makes you break more easily. We've got a more urgent problem. What are we gonna do?"

"Nothing. We go on like it didn't happen. If it happens again, we deal with it."

"I don't know if the captain is going to bounce back to his old self," Rusty said. "His decision-making might become erratic from here on out. If it happens, we might have to deal with that too."

"If it happens." Charlie had no interest in taking on the captain, who imposed a godlike will upon the submarine and its crew. In any case, the "rocks and shoals"—the Articles for the Government of the United States Navy—contained no specific provisions for removing a captain at sea.

He added, "We could be court-martialed for even talking about it."

"He's tired. We're all tired. But we have to keep at it. One more big push." Rusty sighed. "I just wish Cooper had given you command."

"It's easy to judge. It's the toughest job on the boat. You know…"

"What?"

"When Cooper said he'd given it to Howard Saunders, I felt relief."

Rusty said, "You're scared of the job. Everybody is. The truth is you're ready for it."

"You think so?"

"Half the job is knowing what you're doing. The other half is acting at all times like you know what you're doing. You've already proven you're a fast learner, you're aggressive, and you can keep your head in a crisis."

"Well," Charlie said. He never was any good at taking a compliment and didn't know what to say. "When I make captain, maybe you'll be my XO."

Rusty yawned. "Maybe I will, brother."

"What do you think the best quality is for a captain?"

His friend didn't answer. A moment later, he was snoring.

Charlie rolled onto his side and stared at the bulkhead in the gloom. Every submarine captain had his own unique personality and style. He wondered what kind of commander he would be. How well he would handle the pressure. Captain Saunders' successes marked him as a submarine ace. The man once had nerves of steel, but even steel grew fragile if worn down enough. He'd warred so long he was now at war with himself, just like his acey-deucey game.

In one way, Saunders reminded Charlie of Gilbert Moreau. Like all submarine aces, they were both part bulldog. Once they smelled blood, they bit down and never let go. Like Captain Mush Morton had said, stay with the bastard until he's on the bottom. But instead of a desire to see an ultimate end to the war, hatred motivated Moreau. That hatred drove him to take bigger and bigger risks with his boat and crew, which he considered chips in a deadly high-stakes poker game.

In another way, the captain reminded him of Bob Hunter, commander of the *Sabertooth*. Hunter had a competent mind and a good heart, and his crew loved him. He believed a commander optimized his chances by grabbing every advantage from the luck of the draw. But his torpedoes didn't work, and his resulting failures broke him. Similarly, the loss of the *Flagfin* had broken Saunders.

Charlie had learned a lot from all of them. His greatest mentor, however, remained his first commander. Captain J.R. Kane, the chess player. Kane was patient, decisive, cool in combat, and even-handed with his crew. He performed a miracle with an old, broken-down sugar boat. A bold technician, a rare combination. He didn't fight from hate but from a deep sense of duty, and nothing ever broke him.

One day, Charlie Harrison would join the ranks of these great men. Perhaps soon. He hoped he would live up to their successes and avoid their mistakes. And he prayed he'd be as good as Captain Kane.

Sandtiger's hum at last lulled him toward sleep.

He awoke with a start.

"The O3!" a man was shouting in the dark.

"What?" Rusty cried. "Why are you shaking me?"

"We've got an emergency," the sailor said. "The depth-charging damaged the compressed air tanks. I was told I had to blow the O3 or we'll run out of air."

"Wait. What?"

Charlie suppressed laughter. Just like old times.

"I have to blow the O3, sir!"

O3 was the pay grade designation for lieutenant. Another snipe hunt for one of the greenhorns, courtesy of the boat's biggest asshole.

"Tell Braddock the O3 already drained his ballast tanks in the head," Rusty growled. "Now get lost before I throw you and him overboard for a float test!"

Charlie shook with laughter as the bewildered greenhorn fled the cabin.

"You'd think after almost getting blown up, he'd give it a rest," his friend said.

"You were right about one more thing," Charlie chuckled. "It's the little things that get you through a war."

He closed his eyes and instantly returned to sleep. A hand shook him what felt like minutes later.

Charlie growled, "Damn it, if this is another snipe hunt—"

"We've got a situation, Mr. Harrison," Smokey said.

He rubbed his face. "What's the problem?"

"It's the Scouts. They called us. They want off the island."

CHAPTER SEVENTEEN
MUTINY

Charlie sat up with a groan and checked the time: 0800. "You should be resting, Smokey."

"When I'm dead, Exec."

"You feeling all right?"

The man rubbed his shoulder. "I feel like I was shot out that tube. I'm getting too old for this."

Rusty hopped down from his bunk. "What happened to the Scouts?"

"They requested immediate evac, Mr. Grady."

Charlie put on fresh service khakis and followed Smokey to the conning tower, where the officers convened at the plotting table.

"What's our status?" Charlie said.

Percy pointed to the chart laid out on the table. "I surfaced the boat here off the west coast of Tinian to start repairs, which are still in progress. All mains on propulsion. The battery is fully charged. We're now here, bearing oh-one-five."

Off the east coast of Tinian, heading north by northeast

back to Magicienne Bay. *Sandtiger* would reach it within the hour.

"We're still leaking?"

"Yeah, but the pumps can handle it. If we have to run silent again, we'll have a problem, though."

Percy had everything well in hand here.

"Carry on to the rendezvous." Charlie glanced at Rusty. "I'd better go fill in the captain."

And find out if the man was still fit to command. He hoped Saunders had recovered from his mistake and was learning from it. Then he remembered how Captain Harvey reacted after he'd lost his nerve during *Sandtiger*'s test run.

Rusty nodded past Charlie's shoulder. "You can fill him in here."

Captain Saunders didn't look well. Sweat poured down his face and formed large black stains across his uniform's chest and under his armpits.

Charlie laid everything out before the man could speak. Heading, engines on propulsion, state of battery charge, condition of the boat, and the Scouts' radio message. "We don't know if the Scouts succeeded or failed," he finished. "We're heading to the rendezvous coordinates so we can pull them out at sundown."

"And who decided that, Mr. Harrison? You and Mr. Grady?"

"Yes, Captain."

"That's right. I'm the goddamn captain! And I make

the goddamn decisions on this boat! Such as whether to fool around with a hot torpedo while in combat!"

Across the conning tower, the crew goggled at them before returning to their duties.

There was only one response Charlie could give: "Yes, Captain."

Saunders stabbed his finger at Rusty. "You, Judas. Taking control of the boat behind my back while I was focused on evading that Jap destroyer. And you, Mr. Harrison! Going along with it!"

Rusty wilted under the assault. "We had no choice, sir."

"Mutiny!" the captain bellowed, making the crewmen flinch at their stations.

Charlie fought to contain his anger. "Captain, it was my—"

"Silence!"

He shut up. The captain had gone from wanting to relive his history to actively rewriting it. He'd proven himself unfit for duty. In the rocks and shoals, the words were, "culpably inefficient in the performance of duty," a court-martial offense.

But so was saying a single seditious or mutinous word, creating a Catch-22.

Saunders was captain of this boat, king of this kingdom. Period. He'd made a colossal mistake. He'd broken under stress. Another man might have learned from it and moved on, done better. But that would require forgiveness. He'd have to forgive himself. Saunders wasn't the type. And so he blamed his officers.

"I could have you both arrested and confined to quarters on bread and water," the captain snarled. "I could bust you to Seamen, Second Class! But I won't."

"Thank you, sir."

The captain grinned. "But I will see you both tried by court-martial when we get back to Pearl."

Charlie stepped back, eyes wide in disbelief. Rusty had turned gray. Nixon inched away from the table until his back met the TDC. Percy glanced from the captain to Charlie in amazement.

Captain Saunders' eyes swept the conning tower as if daring anybody to challenge his authority, which remained absolute. "I have the conn," he said. "Helm, steady as you go. We've got to rescue some Scouts."

The helmsman nodded, his face pained. "Aye, aye."

"Mr. Ellis," he barked. "Tell the Scouts to be ready to disembark. We'll make contact as soon as we reach the bay."

The radioman stared at him in surprise. "Aye, aye," he stammered.

"Mr. Nixon! Quit your hiding and give me a damage report."

"Captain," Charlie said. "It's daylight."

"And I say we're going to get those Scouts out now, Mr. Harrison. While you and Mr. Grady practice staying out of my sight."

"Aye, aye, Captain."

He and Rusty retreated down to the control room. Charlie moved without awareness of his body, as if in a nightmare. Then he bumped his elbow against a protruding lever, and the jolt of pain snapped him out of it.

Rusty was still pale. From fear or rage, Charlie couldn't tell.

"The captain—"

Charlie held his finger to his lips. "I'm sorry I got you into this."

"Don't be sorry for saving our lives. And don't forget I was the one who got you into all this."

A headache bloomed in his skull. "I need a cup of coffee."

"I'm buying," Rusty said.

In the wardroom, they poured mugs of hot coffee and sat at the small table bolted to the deck. If Saunders pressed his claim, they were in deep trouble. The captain's word against theirs. In a trial like this, a captain, especially one with Saunders' reputation, would have the stronger say.

Charlie doubted a court comprised of senior officers would publicly agree one of their own had shown dereliction of duty because of a mental breakdown.

After this patrol, Charlie might be stripped of rank and pay, thrown off the submarines, or worse. He might be imprisoned. He might even be shot.

Regardless of the outcome, he'd never make captain. He was finished in the submarines.

They sat quietly. There was nothing to talk about other than the captain's erratic behavior and their doom, and they weren't allowed to talk about either. Rusty stared at the dull wood wall paneling while his coffee cooled. Charlie drained his own mug and refilled it before returning to his seat.

Percy entered the room and said, "Christ! The Old Man's a maniac."

Charlie swept his finger across his throat. In a submarine, the bulkheads had ears. Percy shrugged and dropped onto one of the chairs.

"Who cares?" the torpedo officer said. "We're about to surface a leaking submarine in shallow Japanese waters in broad daylight. He's trying to kill us."

"Percy," Charlie warned.

"What about you? You guys all right?"

He thought about it. "I don't know how to answer that."

"It's better if we don't talk for a while," Rusty said.

"I knew things were going to hell when I wasn't allowed to wear my Aloha shirts," Percy said. "Well, if you can't say it, play it."

The officer reached behind him and pulled out his banjo case. He removed the banjo and tuned it. He strummed some chords, which settled into "Blue Moon."

After a while, he said, "Join in anytime, fellas."

Charlie sat fuming. Then he said, "Screw it."

He took out his harmonica, puckered his lips around the tin, and blew through the number six hole, using his tongue to block the five. From there he entered the melody, drawing out the long notes with a wah-wah produced by waving his hand. Percy laughed and played a countermelody.

"Shit," Rusty said, taking out his fiddle and joining in.

The result was beautiful as it always was, and Charlie lost himself and his cares in the music.

Smokey walked into the wardroom livid with fury. "I'll testify—"

The officers ignored him. Charlie appreciated his support but knew, even if the whole crew testified, they'd only hurt their careers and very likely wouldn't affect the outcome. He blanked out his mind again and kept playing.

Waldron, the wardroom steward, came in next and crooned the words to the song in his deep, gravelly voice. Spike arrived sputtering, followed by the rest of the chiefs. By the end of the song, a crowd had gathered. Members of the crew who'd come to offer their support and stayed to listen.

This was the part of the service Charlie would miss most of all.

CHAPTER EIGHTEEN
'THE ONLY GOOD JAP...'

Back in Magicienne Bay. Charlie scrutinized the approaching raft from the *Sandtiger*'s bridge.

"It's Cotten," he said. "He's alone. I don't see the rest of his guys."

Charlie hoped the man hurried it up. They were completely exposed in bright tropical sunlight.

"What happened?" Smokey said.

"I don't know."

Charlie found it hard to think about anything other than getting the Scout aboard and going deep before the Japanese spotted them.

Heaving at the oars, the Scout came close enough for Charlie and Smokey to haul him aboard. Gasping, the man collapsed on the bridge. Smokey stabbed the rubber raft with a knife and let it sink. Charlie crouched next to the lieutenant.

"Where are your men, Jonas?"

"Get out of here," Cotten said. "Dive the boat."

Charlie didn't need to be told twice. "Give me a hand with him, Smokey."

They dragged him to the hatch and passed him inside before dropping down to the conning tower. The quartermaster called out the hatch was secured.

"Planes, take us to periscope depth!" Captain Saunders snapped. "Lt. Cotten! Where's the rest of your team?"

"Dead," the Scout said. "Or good as dead. I think they grabbed Moretti."

The Japanese could already guess a submarine had brought the Scouts to the island. If the Japanese captured one of Cotten's men, eventually they'd make him talk. Then they'd know exactly where the submarine was.

Charlie stared at the captain, hoping the man understood the even greater danger they were now in. Saunders blinked in comprehension.

"Helm, turn us about," the captain ordered. "Come to oh-nine-oh."

"Aye, aye, Captain."

"Planes, stand by to go deep once we clear the bay!"

Charlie blew a relieved sigh. They were submerged and moving. It was time to put as much distance as they could between *Sandtiger* and the Japanese.

"What about the gun?" Captain Saunders asked the Scout. "The Meteor? You didn't have time to destroy it."

Cotten hung his head. "We never even got a look at it."

They'd failed.

In a short time, tens of thousands of Marines would stream toward the beaches in tracked landing vehicles. All under aimed fire, including the Meteor's devastating barrage. Each shot striking earth and sea like the hand of God.

"Mr. Harrison!" Saunders said. "Get him below."

"Aye, Captain."

Charlie got Cotten into the wardroom and sat him in one of the chairs. Rusty handed him a cup of coffee, which he held untasted.

"What happened?" Rusty said.

"There was a boy."

"Go ahead," Charlie encouraged.

The Scout's glazed eyes flickered and focused. "They're dead because of me. Like it was me pulling the trigger."

Rusty produced a battered notepad from his breast pocket. "Start at the beginning."

"They're dead. There's nothing else."

"He's been through hell," Charlie said. "Maybe we should let up on him. Give him a chance to rest and collect himself."

His friend shot him a sharp look. "I'm debriefing him now."

Doing his job. His operation had failed, and he wanted to know why.

"We landed and climbed up the bluff," Cotten said. His eyes blazed as they gazed inward. "Got ourselves oriented and pushed inland. Jungle, sugarcane fields, a stream that wasn't on the maps. We circled around Tsutsurran, sticking to the jungle."

The Scouts came upon a wide patch of open ground.

Two miles of dense grass dotted with brush and low scrub trees. Stars winking overhead. Wearing civilian clothes to blend with the locals, Moretti and Parks blazed a trail ahead. Tropical birds squeaked and screeched in a never-ending chorus from the pandanu trees.

The men signaled all clear. The rest of the squad moved out.

"We made it halfway across when we heard the patrol," Cotten said, his eyes glazing over again as if reliving a dream. "Our luck just got worse from there."

A line of Japanese soldiers hoofed it along a trail that cut through the tall grass. The lieutenant at the front of the column marched smartly, as if on parade. His men followed carrying Arisaka rifles. A full-strength platoon, about fifty men.

The Scouts hunkered down in the grass until invisible. The Japanese tramped past with a clatter of gear. Despite the air raids and meager rations, the soldiers looked fit and ready to fight.

More important to the Scouts, they didn't appear to be searching for the enemy. They seemed bored. Going through the motions. Patrolling friendly ground because somebody higher up told them to.

At last, the platoon faded west into the darkness. Cotten gazed at the sky. Dawn soon. Waiting out the patrol had eaten up a lot of precious time. They had to get under cover and quick.

The lieutenant started to rise when Singer threw him hand signals that said, *Trouble coming, stay down, stay quiet.*

"We heard voices," he said. "Getting louder by the second. Soon, they'd be right on top of us. We hugged the ground and waited."

Cotten expected stragglers, but it was a group of locals. Not Chamorros native to the island; the Japanese government had forcibly relocated most of them years ago. These people were Japanese civilians who'd settled here to grow sugarcane.

The civilians trudged past wearily, carrying machetes and shovels. A work detail, most likely building bunkers for the island's defenders. They'd been working all night and were going home to Tsutsurran.

They too passed. Only a few minutes of darkness left. Singer rose first and gave the all-clear. Then Cotten stood and saw a boy.

"Just some stupid Jap boy," he said. "He was looking right at Ahuli, and he was standing rock still and looking right back. We all just stood there frozen."

Gripping a K-bar in his hand, Cotten worked his way around. He'd taken the lives of a dozen men with this knife during his missions around the Pacific. Each time, he knew if he didn't eliminate them, he and his men would have been killed.

Guided by the same simple calculus, he crept up behind the boy.

Ahuli smiled at the kid. Waved and said hello in Japanese.

"That was my cue," Cotten said. "The only good Jap is a dead Jap, right? But I didn't move. I couldn't do it. I got three kids of my own. One a little girl about that boy's age. He didn't deserve it."

The kid screamed for help.

Gaijin! Gaijin! Gaijin—

Cotten dove and knocked him to the ground. Clamped his hand over the boy's mouth. The Scouts materialized from the tall grass around him.

What now, Singer had whispered.

Wait, he'd answered. *Nobody might have heard. Fan out, and stay low.*

The kid gaped up at him, tears pouring from his eyes.

Voices. The rattle of gear. The Japanese soldiers were returning.

"They had us cut off from retreat," Cotten intoned. "Ahead lay the village the platoon had come out of, crawling with enemy troops. Any minute, fifty Japs were going to be right on top of us. We had to go north."

A man shouted in Japanese. A rifle cracked.

Then the ground jumped as a deafening boom split the air. In the flash of light, Cotten glimpsed a legless soldier cartwheeling through the air. Ahuli opened fire with his Thompson from the north. Muzzle flashes in the grass. The soldiers fell back in confusion, shooting wildly in the dark.

A bugle call rang out. A flare burst overhead.

"I heard some of you guys talk about depth-charging and how it messes with your mind. For most Army guys, it's shelling. For me, it's that goddamn bugle. Freezes the blood in my veins no matter how hot it is. It means slaughter."

The bugle galvanized the soldiers. Bristling with bayonets, a line of howling khaki-clad men charged. Ahuli screamed a Cherokee war cry back at them as the Scouts fired and leapfrogged north, dropping grenades as they went.

Dawn came fast, brightening the sky.

The gunfire rose to a rolling roar. Tracers flashed across the smoky field. A Nambu machine gun rattled. Another bugle call. The soldiers charged again. The civilians returned and joined the charge with their machetes.

Cotten stopped talking.

"And then what?" Rusty said. "Lieutenant?"

He stared into empty space, reliving their final stand in his head now. He winced at the memory.

"And then my men died," he said.

"You tried," Saunders said.

Charlie turned, surprised to see the captain there. Saunders crossed the room to the broken soldier. Rested his hand on the Scout's shoulder and squeezed.

The captain said, "How would you like to try again?"

CHAPTER NINETEEN
SUICIDE MISSION

The officers gaped at the captain.

"What are you proposing, Captain?" Rusty said.

"I'm proposing you go back," Saunders told Cotten.

The lieutenant put his mug of coffee on the table and leaned on his knees, as if he found the very idea exhausting. "You're crazy, sir."

"In three days, Fifth Fleet will land the Fifth Amphibious Corps on the beaches. And that gun will kill a whole lot more good men than you lost today."

Cotten flinched but said nothing.

"You made a mistake," the captain went on. "You can fix it."

"Jesus," Rusty said. "You don't really—"

"I'm asking you to finish the job," Saunders said. "Is it possible?"

"Anything is possible," the Scout said. "It's our other motto." He grimaced. "That and, 'Remember.'"

But it wasn't possible, not by a long shot. Charlie didn't see how one man could return to the island and succeed where six had failed. Especially since they'd stirred up the hornet's nest and let the Japanese know they were there.

Besides that, if what Cotten feared was true, one of the Scouts had been captured. And Cotten was right; he would talk. The Japanese would torture him until he did. Sooner or later, he'd tell the Japanese anything they wanted to hear.

The missing sixth man, the mission to blow up the gun, everything.

If Cotten went back, it was a suicide mission for nothing.

The Scout seemed to understand all this. With his drawn face and downcast eyes, he still looked broken. Then his face slowly transformed as he met the captain's gaze.

Charlie started in surprise. "You're considering it."

"I'd need some help," the man said.

"What would you need?" Saunders said.

"Three of your men ought to do it."

Rusty cut in, "No way. We'd just be throwing away four more lives."

"That's enough out of you, Mr. Grady," Saunders growled.

"He's right, Captain," Charlie said. "They'll never get near the gun."

He winced as Saunders wheeled on him, expecting a drubbing.

"Mr. Harrison, you have combat experience," the

captain said. "Invaded Mindanao with a rubber boat and a Thompson."

Charlie swallowed hard. "Yes, sir."

"That engine snipe went with you. The big man. Braddock. What happened?"

"We went ashore and engaged—"

"I read Hunter's report."

The report said he and Braddock had killed or wounded at least ten enemy soldiers on that beach, which was true. Though only part of the story.

"If you read the report, you know we surprised them then got the hell out of there as fast as we could," Charlie said. "We barely made it out alive."

"You can take Smokey with you. Crack shot with a rifle."

Cotten nodded approval. Charlie exchanged a glance with Rusty, who'd turned white as a sheet. Both Saunders and Cotten had become infected with the same madness. Throwing themselves into danger to get their chance to rewrite their story. Not caring who they dragged into danger with them.

"It's my op, Captain," Rusty said. "I'm calling it off."

"And it's my boat, Mr. Grady! Dismissed! Get out of my sight!"

Rusty opened his mouth to protest further. Closed it when he caught Charlie shaking his head. Saunders was the captain. While it was Rusty's op, the captain's authority on his submarine was absolute.

He left the room shaking.

"Captain, report to the conn," the 1MC blared.

Saunders squared off with Charlie. "You think about your duty, Mr. Harrison."

"Sir, we're not trained—"

"You accomplish the mission, I see a long career for you in the submarines. I see you commanding this boat. I see your friend Grady keeping his job."

Then he stormed from the room to return to the conning tower, leaving Charlie alone with Cotten.

"It's a one-way trip," Charlie said.

"Every trip is a one-way trip in this war. Unless you make it back."

"You get my people killed, the Japs will be the least or your worries. We're not pawns so you get revenge or make things right with yourself. Understood?"

The Scout said, "I'll take care of your people like they're my own."

If Charlie joined their madness, the captain would erase his failures, Cotten would earn his redemption, and he and Rusty would avoid a court-martial.

Everybody would get what they wanted.

As long as he made it back.

He said, "Your captured man—"

"Staff Sergeant Moretti."

"If he talks, they'll know we're going for the gun. They'll be waiting for us. It's bad enough the Japs know we're doing special ops on the island."

"It ain't about 'if,'" Cotten said. "He's gonna tell the Japs nothing, then he'll tell them every little thing they want to know."

"That doesn't sound assuring."

"We train to avoid breaking as long as we can. Until Moretti breaks, the Japs will think we were going after the airfield to blow a supply dump. In fact, that's what he's gonna tell them when he does break. Torture don't work because the intel is always unreliable. We can take out that gun."

"Christ," Charlie said. "You talk about this as if it's all routine."

The Scout shrugged. "It's part of the job."

"Get some food in you, Jonas. Try to rest. Think it over. If we're doing this, we're going tonight at sundown. I need to let the captain know what I've decided."

As if he had a choice.

Charlie mounted to the conning tower and sensed the tense atmosphere at once. The captain leaned over the radarman at his station. The sweat stains had spread down his back, revealing his mental strain.

Saunders turned. "You have an answer for me, Mr. Harrison?"

"We'll go tonight, Captain."

"Very well."

Charlie studied the PPI, which had filled with blips. "What gives?"

"Fifth Fleet, approaching our area of operations,"

Saunders said. "Carrying 70,000 jarheads who will have hell to pay if you don't destroy that gun."

CHAPTER TWENTY
LAST SUPPER

Sandtiger slowly circled off the east coast of Saipan, waiting for midnight.

Charlie returned to the wardroom sweltering in his combat fatigues. Gear belted around his waist, face blackened with grease paint. Thompson slung and pockets bulging with spare magazines. His boots clomped the deck. He felt twice as big and three times heavier than he did in his service khakis.

Similarly dressed for combat, Smokey and Braddock sat with Cotten at the table, upon which Waldron had laid out sandwiches and a pot of fresh coffee. Seeing his shipmates geared up like this surpassed strange.

The machinist glared at him. "Well, sir, you have finally found a sure-fire way to get me killed in this war. Congratulations."

"Stow it, Braddock," Smokey growled. "We're about to go into combat. You'll be relying on Mr. Harrison with your life."

"That goes both ways," Braddock said.

In the machinist's mind, Charlie had the same madness as the captain and Cotten. A lust for going above and beyond one's duty to prove a point while dragging everybody else along for the ride.

Charlie couldn't say out loud that, for once, he agreed with Braddock. The whole thing was nuts. He grabbed a chair, picked up a bacon sandwich, and took a bite. It turned to paste in his dry mouth. He forced himself to swallow.

Cotten checked Charlie's kit. Two Mark II frag grenades, AN-M14 incendiary grenade, M15 Willie Peter grenade, holstered Colt .45, canteen, K-rations, medical packs, 200 rounds for his Thompson, knife, flares, compass.

"Everything is in order," the Scout said. "How are you?"

"Strange, wearing another man's uniform."

"You're wearing his uniform," the Scout said. "You ain't filling his shoes."

Cotten had no idea how right he was about that.

All day, the Scout taught them the basics of his trade. Concealment. Hand signals. Tactics. How to walk, see, and hear in a new way. Stop, look, listen. Watch your interval, move only when the man in front of you is moving, and nobody shoot unless Cotten shoots first.

Then they went over the plan again and again.

When the subject of civilians came up, Cotten said he'd take care of it. Then they'd broken off to grab some quick shut-eye before they left the boat.

In his shipmates, Charlie saw two very capable seamen who still knew nothing about soldiering. This time, Braddock was right. The odds of them succeeding were horrible. Of getting back, almost non-existent.

Cotten asked, "Everybody take your Atabrine pills?"

Atabrine would protect them against malaria. The men nodded and ate in a funereal silence as if awaiting their execution. Right now, malaria was the least of their worries.

Charlie checked the time. The stand of the tide neared. As much as he feared leaving the boat, he just wanted it over with.

"*Alamo team to the conn,*" the 1MC blatted.

"That's us," Cotten said. "Saddle up."

"Just remember," Charlie told Smokey and Braddock. "As soon as we're off the boat, Lt. Cotten is in command. What he says goes."

"I'll get all y'all through this," the Scout said.

No platitudes. No promises of glory, how they'd all come back heroes. What he said was exactly what they needed to hear. That they'd come back in one piece.

The crew turned out to see them off, crowding the control room. The Alamo team marched through them, Smokey leading the way yelling, "Make a hole! Working Navy!"

Charlie's gaze clung to everything he saw before losing its grip and slipping past. He knew every detail of this boat now, every dial and gauge, every quirk and habit. Sometimes, she felt like a metal coffin, her bulkheads closing in and trapping him somewhere deep from which he'd never escape. Most of the time, she felt like a mother's warm womb, like home.

Charlie had a feeling he'd never see her again.

The sailors gawked at their shipmates loaded out for combat. Some shouted encouragement while the rest just stared.

"Make a hole!" Smokey barked.

They mounted to the conn. The captain grinned while the other officers gaped, their faces pale and taut.

"You ready for this, Charlie?" Rusty said.

Charlie pulled on his Mae West lifejacket. "Ready as I can be. Able is another matter."

"If things get dicey, you run like hell and get back here."

He offered a grim smile. Things were already looking pretty dicey to him. "Do you still have it?"

The letter he'd written for Evie on the S-55. *I'm sorry. I love you. Be happy.* He wrote it the night the 55 approached the Japanese fortress of Rabaul. Rusty had penned one just like it to his wife Lucy and given it to Charlie to keep.

Rusty nodded. "It's in my locker. I've gotten pretty attached to it, so don't do anything stupid like making me send it."

"I'll do my best."

The captain ordered the boat to surface. *Sandtiger* rose on an even keel. The hatch opened overhead.

Rusty shook his hand. "Good luck, brother."

"Good hunting, Mr. Harrison!" Captain Saunders said. "Wish I was going with you."

Rusty gave Charlie a look that said he wished the captain was leaving as well. Charlie snorted and began to climb the rungs.

Saunders might be crazy—a man broken by the war, a man who was now trying to use the war to mend himself. That didn't detract from the importance of the mission. Charlie could almost see it in his mind. Fifth Fleet floating outside the barrier reef. Waves of LVTs racing toward the beaches. The Meteor booming and smashing everything in sight with its giant shells.

Charlie wasn't optimistic about his chances, but he knew where he stood on whether the mission was worth personal risk. It was. Destroying that gun would save far more lives than might be paid for trying.

Somebody had to do it. Somebody had to try. He steeled his nerve as he mounted to the bridge.

Maybe Braddock was right, and he was crazy too.

Her decks awash, the submarine lay partially surfaced under a rising moon. Two sailors inflated a raft. Cotten, Smokey, Braddock, and Charlie climbed in and grabbed paddles. The sailors waved before disappearing down the hatch.

"Ready." Cotten pointed where he wanted the raft to go.

As the bow paddlers, he and Charlie started the

strokes. Smokey and Braddock joined in, matching their pace. Charlie spared a quick glance over his shoulder, hoping to catch a final glimpse of the *Sandtiger*.

The submarine sank into the foam. No going back now.

Ahead lay the limestone cliffs of Saipan's eastern shore.

CHAPTER TWENTY-ONE
THE CLIFFS

Charlie matched Cotten's rigorous rowing pace across the slack water. *Sandtiger* had made her presence known in these very waters earlier in the day, and the moon was out and rising.

"Dig," Cotten rasped. "Hard forward! Dig!"

Until they reached the cliffs, they were sitting ducks. At any moment, Charlie expected a Nambu machine gun to open fire from the bluff.

"Deliver us from evil," Smokey prayed in the back. "Deliver us—"

The men lurched as an invisible hand grabbed the boat. Charlie tottered, raising his arms to maintain balance.

The raft began to spin.

"Sleeper," Smokey called out.

The raft was hung up on a rock hiding under the water's surface.

Cotten grunted agreement. "We need to boogie."

"What?" said Charlie.

"Bounce around! We need to shake loose."

The men bounced in the raft, slowly working it off the rock until it spun off across the surface. They hacked at the water until they regained control and had the raft aimed once again at the distant cliffs.

"Now dig!" Cotten barked. "Watch your trim! Hard forward!"

The raft approached the volcanic rock piled at the base of the cliffs. Cotten hauled himself onto a boulder and belayed the raft using a line pulled taut through an anchor. Working by moonlight, the rest of the team piled out with their gear.

Then the moon dimmed to black. The humid air grew even heavier, pregnant with rain. Braddock deflated the raft and wedged it into his pack.

"We'd better do this quick," Cotten said. "I'll go up first."

Smokey gazed up the face of the chalky cliffs, his head tilting back and his mouth open. "That's really high."

"It looks higher than it is," Charlie said as he observed the Alamo Scout's progress. Cotten was already a quarter of the way to the top, hauling himself up using the rope he'd left behind.

"You afraid of heights, Chief?" Braddock sneered.

"As a matter of fact, I am," Smokey said. "Just looking at them makes me want to punch somebody."

For once, the machinist shut up when he should. Light flickered overhead, and they flinched. Thunder crackled seconds later.

Charlie blew out a sigh. "Can you make the climb?"

"I don't know, sir. I really don't."

"You could have said something on the boat," Braddock said.

Smokey glared at him as if wondering whether he'd deliver that punch now or later. "It doesn't look that high from a distance."

"Braddock, you go up next," Charlie said. "Tell the lieutenant we're going to haul Smokey up with a fly walk."

"Aye, aye." Braddock grabbed the rope. "Looks like I'll be carrying your ass the whole way up, Chief."

"Get your own ass moving before I kick it up there."

"Aye, aye." Braddock started pulling.

"Still wondering why you brought him along," Smokey muttered.

Right now, Charlie had no good answer.

After the engine snipe made it to the top, Charlie wrapped the rope around the quartermaster's armpits and tied it off. "I saw people doing this at Glen Canyon once. Cotten and Braddock will pull you up."

"You're shitting me."

Charlie tugged on the rope to tell the men above Smokey was ready. "Just walk up at the same pace they pull," he said. "You'll be at the top in no time. When you get there, keep your uppermost leg straight and rigid to act as a lever."

The rope went taut. Smokey placed his boot against

the rock and started walking up the cliff face. Another flash of light whitened the sky, followed by a crash.

"Our father!" he yelled.

"Just keep walking, you'll be fine," Charlie called after him.

"Deliver us from evil!"

Smokey made it to the top and disappeared. The rope dropped and swayed. Charlie grabbed it and started hauling himself up. At first, the going was difficult against the slippery rock. His boot soles rasped against limestone formed by the skeletons of tiny marine organisms built up over millions of years. Calcium carbonate. Crumbs of it trickled down the cliff side.

A creature clicked and growled at him. A cliff bird, which Charlie knew was a masked booby, rustled in its cave, protecting its young.

"Just passing through," he gasped.

The world went white.

He huddled half-blind against the rock. The air around him roared. Disoriented, he wondered if Fifth Fleet had started shelling the island.

A heavy drop of water splatted against his jungle cap. Another. Charlie hauled himself up with renewed energy, making every second count.

Wind blasted down the cliff face. Then the rain rushed down in buckets, pushing against him like a living thing. Water sluiced into his eyes, nose, and mouth. It soaked into his gear and boots. In seconds, sheets of it poured down the cliff like a waterfall.

The rope slid in his gloved hands. He tightened his grip and held on through sheer force of will, pulling himself up step by step against the deluge. His boot slipped, and he hung free as the men above hauled him up. He regained purchase with his feet and kept going, one pull followed by the next. His arms burned with exertion as they approached their limit.

Another heart-stopping flash of light, followed by a rolling avalanche of thunder. Hands lifted him by the armpits and dragged him onto a bed of grass, where he lay gasping as the rain poured down.

Unable to see more than a few feet in any direction, he crawled away from the edge. The other men were vague dark shapes behind a wall of rain.

Trembling with exhaustion, he pulled off his Mae West. They'd barely started the mission, and already Charlie was spent. The storm brought misery but also respite. They'd wait it out and rest up.

A shape appeared in his path. Eyes burning against a blackened face.

"On your feet, soldier," Cotten shouted over the gale. "We're moving out!"

CHAPTER TWENTY-TWO

BAPTISM

The violent storm pounded the jungle.

Charlie crept along the muddy game trail. He couldn't see Cotten on point. For what felt like hours, they'd sneaked across a plateau tangled with underbrush and dotted with giant boulders.

When they'd reached the jungle, the Scout's instruction had been simple: follow the trail. Surrounded by sheets of water falling from the jungle canopy, Charlie felt like he walked alone.

Then the rain stopped as abruptly as it had begun.

He froze, feeling exposed, and wiped water from his eyes. Cotten was waving at him. *Get off the trail now. Pass it along.*

Charlie turned and waved Smokey and Braddock off the trail. Dripping, he slogged into the ferns. Water condensed in the hot night air. Fog rose all around him as he pushed into the thick undergrowth, trying to keep an eye on the Scout.

Then Cotten disappeared. Charlie floundered after him. If they lost the lieutenant, they were finished.

The Scout reached from the darkness and gripped his arm. Held his finger to his lips. *Keep quiet. Follow me.*

Charlie stopped to rest his hands on his knees, sucking in the thick, humid air. He pulled as much of it into his lungs as he could and walked slowly in the Scout's trail, one eye on Cotten, the other on the ground.

And much, much quieter.

With the rain stopped, the air filled with mosquitoes. The insects hummed around him. He knew better than to slap at them, which would produce noise. He rubbed them off his face, only to feel another nagging sting. Charlie brushed at them with his gloved hands until rage burned in his chest.

What I am doing here?

Make it your friend, he told himself. *The rain, the exhaustion, the mosquitoes. Embrace it. Own it.*

He waved a whining insect away from his ear.

Cotten was frantically signaling him. *Get down!*

He passed on the signal and lowered himself quietly onto the mud. Behind him, Smokey and Braddock sank into the fog like ghosts.

Voices. The clatter of gear.

A thought nagged at him.

He was lying on a patch of ground that had no plants growing from it.

Another game trail. In moments, the Japanese would march right up to him.

Charlie rolled into a tangle of ground vines as the voices grew louder and boots splashed in the mud.

A black shape materialized from the mist. A rain-soaked Japanese soldier in khaki uniform. Field cap with a neck flap, tunic, trousers with shins wrapped in puttees. Ammunition belt and pouches, canteen, bayonet, long Arisaka bolt-action rifle. Water vapor misted off him as he approached.

Once again, Charlie found himself within shooting distance of one of the toughest fighters in the world. The Japanese infantryman rarely ran, never surrendered, and would charge even if it meant certain death.

Charlie's heart crashed in his ears. He wondered if the soldier could hear it.

Mud splashed his face as the soldier tramped past, followed by another. A file of riflemen. A section, about fifteen men. They grumbled as they marched.

A man stopped directly in front of Charlie. Strange boots with a split toe that made his feet look like hooves. Charlie shifted his eyes to look up.

The soldier gazed right back at him.

Charlie started to reach for his K-bar but froze. The soldier's rifle remained slung over his shoulder. He fidgeted with his trousers.

A warm stream splatted against Charlie's back.

He shut his eyes but otherwise remained still. Cotten had told him a man couldn't see another in the dark unless he moved.

Think about something else, he told himself. *Anything else.*

A dozen memories sprang into his mind, but none held. The steady splatter between his shoulder blades blocked out any thought except disgust and fury.

That and pure terror the soldier would realize what he was urinating on.

At last, the stream stopped. The soldier sniffed the air once, twice. His head lowered to peer into the undergrowth where Charlie lay hidden.

A man called out in Japanese. The soldier raised his head and responded. Then he trudged after his section.

The jungle silenced except for the ring of insects. Something crawled across Charlie's hand, but still he didn't move, his body clenched with fear.

Cotten made a clicking sound. Charlie rose and followed the Scout deeper into the jungle, maintaining a five-yard interval.

He expected his legs to be shaky, but wrath had replaced his terror. He'd steamed halfway around the world to get pissed on. He wanted to blow up that gun and make this all worth something.

Dawn arrived with alarming suddenness. The team huddled around the Scout, who shrugged off the thirty-five-pound SCR-300 radio he'd carried on his back and sat against the trunk of a red-orange flame tree.

"All y'all did good," he said. "We'll hold up here for an hour."

"What happens after that?" Charlie said.

Cotten checked his compass and put it back in his breast pocket. "A hundred meters or so to the north, there should be a stream. We'll find a nice secluded spot to wait. When night comes, we'll refill our canteens and cross over."

"The island's crawling with Japs," Smokey said.

"We're gonna take it real slow. Real slow and real quiet."

"How far is the gun now?" Charlie said.

"I reckon we made around two klicks last night, which ain't bad, considering. We'll assault the gun tonight after it gets dark."

Two kilometers inland. Right now, they were directly between Tsutsurran, Aslito Airfield, and heavy concentrations of entrenched Japanese troops guarding the island's southwestern beaches.

"What were those soldiers talking about?" Braddock said.

"They were bitching about being out in the rain, their shit rations, and their lousy officers," the Scout answered and took a swig from his canteen. "But that's just a guess. Aside from a few military words, I don't speak Jap."

"They sound a lot like you, Braddock," Charlie said. "If we get captured, I'm sure there's plenty you can all talk about, comparing notes."

"Not me, sir," Braddock said. "I regard my officers as an inspiration."

Charlie snorted at the barb, suddenly aware how thirsty he was. His throat felt like leather. He unscrewed the cap on his canteen and poured the warm water down his throat. The most satisfying drink he ever had.

"Easy on that," Cotten said. "It has to last the day. We can't refill at the stream until it gets dark."

"And wash up too," Braddock told Charlie. "You smell like the head, sir."

"Thanks for your concern."

"Everybody gets scared. Nothing to be ashamed of."

The Scout laughed. "That ain't his piss you're smelling. A Jap stopped and took a whiz right on our friend here. He smelled Charlie's body odor, though."

The men cracked grins. Charlie expected another smart-ass tirade from the machinist, but the man just nodded with something like respect.

"Damn," Smokey said and whistled at how close it all was.

"Charlie," said Cotten, "consider that your baptism. You're a Scout now."

CHAPTER TWENTY-THREE

SACRIFICE

Braddock provided security with his BAR while the others got ready to chow down on their K-rations. Charlie pulled a box from his tunic pocket labeled, US ARMY FIELD RATION K, BREAKFAST.

Chopped ham and eggs in a can, biscuits, malted milk tablets, dried fruit bar, instant coffee and sugar, Wrigley gum, toilet paper, and Halazone water purification tablets. He ate dutifully, replacing consumed calories, and saved the coffee. They wouldn't be making any fires today.

"Makes you appreciate the chow Uncle Charlie gets us." Smokey eyed his breakfast doubtfully. "I'll never give the cook a ribbing again."

Vice Admiral Charles Lockwood went above and beyond to ensure the submarines received the best provisions.

"We eat pretty good too," Cotten said. "When we're not in the field."

The men finished their breakfast in silence. Smokey lay on the ground with his head against a tree trunk and fell asleep.

The tropical sun burned off the last of the mist. Through the jungle canopy, Charlie glimpsed Mount Fina Susu, carpeted in green. The 300-foot-high hill loomed over the surrounding countryside.

Somewhere up there, the Meteor maintained its sentinel watch over the waters west of the island. Ready to wreak havoc on the American landings. Tonight, Charlie and his team would have to assault that gun and destroy it.

Submarines often faced long odds. They charged into battle against numerous ships with bigger guns and thicker armor, and they emerged victorious because submarines always had one advantage that proved decisive.

Surprise.

As long as Moretti didn't reveal their true objective, they'd launch their assault tonight with total surprise on their side. Overwhelm the crew, destroy the big gun, and get out.

Cotten caught him staring at the mountain. "We can do it, Charlie."

He nodded. "We don't have a choice."

"We can prevent a lot of boys getting killed. And make my boys' deaths mean something."

Charlie took a swig from his canteen to wash down

his breakfast. It took an act of will not to drain it. "What happened to the kid?"

The Scout said nothing.

"Sorry, I didn't mean—"

"Every other island we been on, lots of times, the locals either helped us or were doing their best to ignore a war was going on. Just trying to live their lives. This was our first mission with Jap civilians. They didn't train us for that."

The Scout picked up his entrenching tool and dug a hole to bury their trash. "I hope the Japs give up before we get to their home islands. I really do. They may not have weapons, but they're soldiers, every one of them. Even the kids."

Charlie pictured the massacre that was to come and wondered if the war would ever end. "They're going to make us kill them all," he said with disgust.

"You got any regrets, Charlie?"

Again, that question from a man who knew something about it.

"I've taken a few big risks that strike me as foolish now," he said. "But I've been lucky."

"While my boys were getting shot up, I stayed on the ground with the kid. The Jap grunts ran right past me. Me and this kid, we just looked at each other. Right in the eye. Me holding my knife, knowing I had to finish it. Him crying."

Cotten's face twisted into a mixture of fury and despair.

Charlie said, "You don't have to tell me. I'm sorry I asked."

"That kid was our Alamo. I actually wanted to kill him for what he done."

"But you didn't, did you?"

"After the fighting was over and the Japs all left, I put up my K-bar. The boy understood. If I let him walk, he'd keep his mouth shut. We made a deal."

"There probably wasn't much you could have done anyway. If you didn't stay hidden, they would have killed you too."

"What's my life worth now?" Cotten's eyes blazed. "I got my boys killed because I didn't cut a kid's throat. What would you have done in my place?"

"I don't know, Jonas." He was no good at this kind of talk. "I'd like to think I wouldn't have killed him either. Part of me wants to think I would to save my men. Either way, I'd probably end up with one hell of a big regret."

"Back home, I was nobody special. I joined the Scouts because I wanted to be the best I could. I wanted to meet myself. Find out what I was really made of. When I had my K-bar out ready to kill that boy, I did."

"You aren't a cold-blooded murderer," Charlie said. "That's a good thing."

"Then I don't belong here." Cotten turned away and wiped his eyes. "This goddamn war. Only the cold-blooded are gonna survive it."

Charlie wished he had the words that might ease

the man's conscience. He doubted any words could. "Sometimes it's just that. The war. Not you—"

A rifle cracked deep in the jungle. Braddock screamed and went down.

"Contact!" Cotten snatched up his M3 grease gun.

Charlie crouched and ran to Braddock, who lay writhing on the ground.

"Fucker shot me," the man growled.

A bullet snapped past Charlie's ear as he located a bloody patch on Braddock's arm. No time to dress it. "It looks like it passed clean through."

"It hurts like hell!"

"Get on your feet! Move it!"

Muzzle flashes in the trees. Charlie fired wildly with his Thompson then helped the sailor up. Together, they ran past their comrades, who laid down suppressing fire before falling back.

"They're gonna try and flank us," the Scout said as they darted through the trees. "We got no choice but to get across the stream."

"They'll shoot us while we cross," Charlie said. "I'll strike east and see if I can draw them off. Meet up with you later."

"No, sir," Smokey said. "I'll do it. You get to the gun."

"Go, Smokey," said Cotten.

Before Charlie could protest, the quartermaster sped off with his Garand.

The Scout was already running toward the stream.

Charlie chased after him, Braddock huffing at his side, nursing his bleeding arm.

Behind them, a Garand popped, followed by the ping of an ejecting clip. Smokey was harassing the Japanese flank, making himself known.

Bright sunlight struck Charlie as the jungle cleared. The stream gurgled, cool and inviting. He splashed into it.

"Go!" Cotten said. "I'll cover forward."

Bracing his legs against the current, Charlie forded the water with big strides. Braddock kept pace alongside him, his face white as a sheet. They flinched as the jungle behind erupted with the crackle of gunfire.

Reaching the other side, they hunkered down in the bushes. Cotten was already coming across while Braddock covered him with the BAR.

Distant booms. Rumbles Charlie felt deep in his chest. Freight trains tore the air overhead. Meteors flamed across the blue sky.

The naval bombardment had begun. Fifth Fleet was in action, a day earlier than scheduled.

The ground trembled as the massive shells struck the island. The next blast knocked him flat. The air shimmered in the south as a vast plume of dirt, entire trees, and the matchstick remains of buildings reached for the sky.

Cotten landed next to him. "Stay down!"

Charlie hugged the ground as Smokey emerged from

the trees on the opposite bank, nursing a wounded arm.

He smiled with relief. "There's Smokey!"

Come on, he thought, willing the chief to go faster. *Run!*

The quartermaster dropped his rifle and raised his left arm.

Khaki-clad soldiers encircled him, screaming over the blasts. Charlie quickly counted thirteen men, nearly a whole section of infantry.

"*Jishu! Jishu!*"

Smokey had taken two of them, and now the rest had caught him. They'd beat him. Torture him. Then they'd execute him.

The ground shook again from the impact of sixteen-inch shells.

Charlie aimed his Thompson. *Not on my watch.*

A strong arm wrapped around his throat, the other reaching across to shove his weapon's barrel into the dirt.

Charlie struggled, but the man held him fast.

"Stop," Cotten hissed in his ear. "He's done. There's nothing we can do."

"The hell we can't," he grunted.

"Smokey knows the score."

"Braddock, fire that BAR. That's an order."

The sailor glanced from Charlie to Cotten and shook his head. "The lieutenant's right, sir. And he's in charge."

"I order you to shoot!"

"The Scout knows what he's doing."

"It's on me," Cotten said. "It's on me, not you."

"Damn you," Charlie raged. He stopped struggling and gaped as the Japanese soldiers closed in on the chief with their bayonets. Another wall of dirt and trees roared over the jungle behind them. The shockwave rippled through the earth.

Smokey exploded.

The grenades he'd been hugging against his body blew him in half. The soldiers around him went down like ragdolls and lay smoking.

"Get up," Cotten growled in his ear. "Get moving."

"Smokey?"

It should have been him.

"He's gone. Come on!"

Charlie wiped his eyes and got back to his feet.

Then he followed Cotten through willows and ground vines into a sugarcane field, thinking all the while he'd finally found one regret that would haunt him.

CHAPTER TWENTY-FOUR

INFERNO

Another salvo smashed into the island and shook the earth. Shells tore the air overhead with metallic screams. Somewhere in the Philippine Sea, massive battleships, including four of the giants damaged during the attack on Pearl Harbor, gave Saipan everything they had.

The Americans burrowed into a narrow tunnel between sugarcane stalks soaring ten feet tall. The fronds pressed in from all sides and blinded them.

Cotten finally stopped. "We'll rest up here a minute."

"I'll see to Braddock," Charlie gasped.

Braddock slumped against a stool of maturing cane stalks. Charlie cut a hole in the sailor's shirt and examined the wound.

"How are you?" he said.

The sailor grit his teeth. "How the fuck do you think I am, sir? I'm shot."

"Then stop moving so I can treat it, you asshole."

"It hurts like hell!"

"It passed clean through the muscle. Now who's lucky?"

"Yeah, look at me," Braddock man. "I'm the luckiest man alive."

Charlie produced a packet of sulfa, tore it open with his teeth, and doused the entry and exit holes. The white powder contained chemicals that controlled infection. In the tropics, without sulfa, infection would kill you if the bullet didn't.

Then he tightly wrapped Braddock's arm in a bandage to stop the bleeding and keep dirt and insects from the wounds. "You'll live."

He tried to smile but failed. Smokey was dead, finally able to truly rest. He pressed his hands against the sides of his head. He was supposed to go, not Smokey.

"It isn't only you, sir," Braddock said. "It never is. You don't get to figure this out just now."

Charlie couldn't win the war by himself. And each time he took risks, so did the men he led into combat.

"You're right," he said. "It isn't just me. There's a war on, and if we don't step up, a lot more Americans are gonna get killed."

"The mission comes before the man," Cotten agreed. "It's why we're here."

Braddock said, "Some of us want—"

"Save it for later," Charlie growled. "We have a job to do. Can you use the BAR?"

The Browning Automatic Rifle weighed about twenty pounds, twice the weight of the Thompson Charlie carried. A powerful weapon with a strong recoil.

"I can handle it," the sailor said. "I see a Jap, I'll put him down for good."

Another salvo howled overhead, sending waves of dirt reaching for the sky. The ground rocked underfoot, knocking them over. Heaved again, flinging them bouncing along the ground.

The sky darkened as a massive dust cloud obscured the sun. Gray smoke encroached on the air around them. Dirt clods rained.

"The field's on fire," the Scout said. "We got to move!"

The farmers did this every year. They set fire to their fields to burn off the leaves and bugs, enrich the soil, and make the surviving cane stalks easier to harvest. But not this time, not now.

The shelling had ignited the field. That or the Japanese knew the Americans were here and were flushing them out into the open like rabbits.

Charlie wrestled against the thick fronds, which wrapped around him as if trying to hold him back. He remembered the checkerboard pattern of cane fields in the grainy recon photos. Each a thousand feet wide.

The smoke thickened. The air grew even hotter. The fire was close and getting closer, its progress checked solely by moisture clinging to the leaves.

Charlie stumbled as another shell crashed in the

distance, and then he was free of the cane field.

Cotten dragged him to the ground. "Down!"

Charlie coughed on the smoke. "Japs?"

The Scout scanned the area with his binoculars. "Looks clear to me. We're gonna stay close to the field and then break for that sugar mill."

They moved quickly along the field's edge and darted to the ruins. The large sugar mill still stood, blackened by soot. The roof over one side had been smashed in by an errant bomb that turned its machinery into a tangle of twisted metal. The other side looked like a charred skeleton.

Communicating with hand signals, the men cleared it and gathered around a body that sat against the wall, legs splayed.

It was Walsh.

The giant's head lay cocked to the side, his sightless eyes aimed up at the sky visible through the holed roof. He'd given himself a field dressing and had tried to complete his mission, but he couldn't make it. Walsh had come here to die.

He'd scrawled a word on the floor with his blood. *GADO.*

"What's that mean?" Charlie asked Cotten.

The Scout's lips compressed into a hard line. "He taught me some Cherokee. It means, 'Why?'"

"Sorry about your man."

"We're all sorry." Cotten yanked his comrade's dog

tags and thumbed his eyes closed. He put his hand over the man's still heart. *"Tsayawesohlvga*. Rest now."

They dug foxholes in the hard dirt floor while the shells kept falling outside. The sugarcane field burned brightly, pumping roiling clouds of thick black smoke into the sky. Then they dug a grave for Walsh and buried him.

This work done, Charlie raised his canteen and chugged greedily. The warm water cleaned his parched and dusty throat.

"Finish that off, and give it here," the Scout said. "I'll be back by dark."

Charlie shook the last few drops onto his tongue and handed over his canteen. "Where are you going?"

Cotten frowned at Walsh's grave.

"Where, Jonas?"

"I'm going back to the stream to refill our canteens."

"We should all go together," Charlie said.

The scout slung the canteens around his neck. "I'll be all right. I move better on my own. Y'all stay and rest."

"What if you don't make it back for some reason?"

"I'm leaving the radio. If I don't make it back, contact your ship. Then y'all can finish the mission or get off the island. Your choice."

"Just make sure you get back."

"Roger that."

As Cotten was leaving, Braddock called out, "Good luck, Lieutenant."

"Call me Jonas," the man said. "We Scouts are an informal bunch."

Then he was gone.

CHAPTER TWENTY-FIVE
INTO HELL

Lying in his foxhole, Braddock snored through the bombardment while Charlie sat by the window eating his lunch, Thompson locked and loaded at his side.

The window offered a stunning view of Mount Fina Susu getting pounded by Navy battleships. Smoke shrouded the mountain from dozens of fires. Chunks of earth sprayed into the air from impacts. The shelling went on until the pulsing roar became part of the background, noticeable only when it paused.

He pitied any soldiers caught out in the open up there.

Did those soldiers know what they were fighting for? He remembered Lt. Tanaka talking about the struggle of nations, empires playing chess for resources and room to grow. The inevitability America and Japan would fight. Charlie doubted the average Japanese soldier understood or cared about all that. The average Japanese fought for his honor and his emperor.

Under this hellish bombardment, it probably all seemed so meaningless now.

Still, they wouldn't give up. Tomorrow, when 70,000 Marines hit the beaches, the Japanese would fight tooth and nail. They'd fight to survive. Isn't that what they were all doing at this point, everyone in this war? Fighting to stay alive?

One thing Tanaka had taught him was that, for the average Japanese soldier, surrender wasn't an option. The only way for him to survive was to win.

Charlie checked his watch. He shook the machinist awake.

"Shit," Braddock said. "I'm still in Saipan."

"How's the arm?"

"Asking me about it isn't going to make it better, sir."

Charlie shrugged and lay in the foxhole to sleep, grateful he'd made it this far, grateful to be alive. And feeling guilty he'd survived when men like Smokey hadn't.

He closed his eyes. Though he'd been running on pure adrenaline all night and morning, sleep eluded him. Again, he played Smokey's death in his mind, trying to find a way it could have gone differently. Wondering if it was all his fault.

Somebody kicked his boot. He sat up with a start. Braddock loomed over him, gnawing on a sugarcane stalk.

Outside the windows, the light was failing.

"Was I asleep?" Charlie mumbled.

"It's 1800, sir."

He rubbed his face. "Where's Cotten?"

"He hasn't come back."

He hauled himself to his feet with a groan. Every part of him ached. "It'll be dark soon. I'll take watch while you get your supper."

"What if he doesn't come back? I guess you'll want to keep going."

Charlie peered through the hole in the wall to inspect the cane field outside, now a smoking ruin. "We can't stay here."

But where to go? Keep going, or head back? They'd only made it this far because of the Scout. On a submarine, they served as part of a war machine that slaughtered ships and men. On land, they were fish out of water.

Untrained and possibly unequal to the task.

"We'll proceed with the mission," he said.

Braddock pulled his K-rations from his pack. "Good."

"And here, I thought you'd be bitching to make a run for it."

"Smokey is on me too," the sailor said. "I didn't shoot. If we blow that gun, maybe he died for something in this stupid war."

A terrific explosion rent the air. The shockwave shook the building. Dust and ash fell from the shattered roof. An American shell had scored a lucky hit on an ammunition dump.

"Right now, I'm worried about us," Charlie said.

"As much as I don't like you, sir, you always try. No

matter how many punches you take, you don't give up. Don't give up now."

Charlie scowled at the scenery, irritated the man's respect pleased him as much as it did. "It'll be dark soon. Get your chow. After that, we'll go blow up that gun."

He wiped sweat from his forehead, feeling an awful thirst. Saipan reminded him of the S-55, where temperatures soared as high as 130 degrees in the engine room, with 100 percent humidity. When the old submarine surfaced and ventilated, which reduced temperature, fog sometimes formed throughout the boat.

The bombardment eased up at sunset. They collected their gear.

"Take a look at this," Charlie said at the door.

Two canteens hung from a nail in the doorframe. Braddock took one down and shook it. "It's full. What does it mean?"

"It means Cotten doesn't need us after all."

The Scout had failed his own squad then lost Smokey despite his promise to Charlie he'd get his people back to the *Sandtiger* safely. Or maybe seeing Walsh's body and final message made him want to go it alone.

Cotten was one of the most capable men Charlie had ever met, but right now, he was being a damned fool.

He'd also taken the satchel charges. All Charlie and Braddock had that could damage the gun was incendiary grenades.

"So what about us?" Braddock said.

Charlie uncapped his canteen and took a long swallow. The water was warm and tasted terrible from the Halazone tablets, but he drank greedily, eyes closed in grateful bliss. He screwed the cap back on. "We're going after him."

Braddock nodded. "Aye, aye."

He glanced at the sailor's arm. "I have to ask."

"Feels like there's a bell in there ringing my brain."

"Can you manage?"

"I'm fine, Mom. Now let's go."

They set out in the darkness toward the hill country surrounding Mount Fina Susu. Silently, mindful of everything the Scout had taught them. They reached the edge of the plateau that dominated the southern part of the island. The land here was covered in scrub trees, brush, and high grass.

The ground sloped upward into hell.

They trudged across torn-up earth carpeted with uprooted trees, giant splinters, and smoking impact craters. Fina Susu glowed like a massive heap of hot coals. Despite the need for quiet, they coughed.

As they gained altitude, the drifting pall of smoke parted. Lake Susupe and its surrounding swamps sprawled at the bottom of the great hill. To the west was the village of Charan Kanoa, dark now. They were close to the coast now, close to the Japanese positions.

Flashes out in the water, followed by booms. Thunder as shells crashed into the area around Tanapag Harbor to the north. Charlie knew the shelling continued to pose an existential threat, though by suppressing Japanese movement, it had also allowed them to progress this far.

Braddock clicked his tongue and pointed at a tangle of smashed 20mm AA guns. Charlie moved that way, sweeping the wreckage with his Thompson.

"Couple of unmarked graves here," the sailor said.

"The rest bugged out. Let's keep moving."

"Wait. Do we know where this big gun is?"

"Yeah," Charlie said. "It's somewhere on this hill."

They just needed to keep going up. The gun would be near the summit, on the west side, facing the barrier reef lagoon.

Braddock gazed up the slope and spat. "Wonderful."

They continued to creep up Fina Susu's scarred face, zigzagging to avoid the heat and light of still-burning fires. Drifting layers of smoke obscured the summit. Between smoke and the darkness, Charlie was marching nearly blind.

Braddock clicked his tongue again. Charlie turned and searched for the sailor behind him.

Then he realized the sound had come from his right.

CHAPTER TWENTY-SIX
ATTACK!

Charlie wheeled, his instincts tingling. Thompson raised and ready to fire.

Instead, he gave the proper answering signal.

Cotten materialized from the tall grass. "I thought I gave you boys a pretty clear out of this."

Charlie shook his head. Too late for that. "I'm glad we found you."

Braddock crept forward. The Scout told them what he'd discovered. A hundred meters from where they crouched in the dense grass, the Meteor stood ready to shoot from a camouflaged, reinforced bunker built into the hill.

From there, its massive gun aimed into the waters off Saipan's western shores.

The casemate was thirty feet wide and likely about thirty feet deep. Gun room, magazine, ventilation, crew's quarters. Around fourteen gunners and guards.

Bad odds, but the Americans still had surprise on their

side. If they hit the Japanese hard and fast, they could sweep the bunker before the enemy could react.

Two doors led inside. The main entrance opened to a guard room. The other an emergency exit. Both carved into the hillside.

"The Japs are on high alert," Cotten said. "We can't attack tonight."

"Then what's the plan?" Charlie said.

"We get under cover fast in case the Navy decides to pound the hill some more. We wait until the Japs start shooting their gun. Then we'll know most of them will be in the gun room and focused on Fifth Fleet."

An armored faceplate protected the Meteor's crew while preventing the enemy from entering the bunker. However, this thick metal plate also featured wide slits used for spotting and small arms defense.

Just wide enough to cram a satchel charge through.

"We'll be making the assault in broad daylight," Braddock said.

"That's right."

The sailor sighed. "Wonderful."

Cotten passed him a satchel containing four tetrytol TNT blocks with an M1 pull-fuse igniter. "You take the front. Me and Charlie will take out the machine gun at the entrance and mop up from there."

"Aye, aye."

Cotten glanced at Charlie's Thompson. "You any good with that?"

"Not really."

Braddock snorted. "You should have seen him on Mindanao. There wasn't a tree left alive after he was done shooting."

"It don't matter," Cotten said. "We'll be in close quarters."

"We only have a few hours of darkness left," Charlie said, not wanting to think about shooting men at point-blank range.

"Let's get into position," said Cotten. "John, once that gun starts booming, you know what to do. We'll hear the TNT go off. That'll be our signal."

Charlie said, "One more thing, Jonas. From here on out, we're in this together. We all want to be here. That's how it is."

"Even if we're not thrilled about it," Braddock added.

The Scout offered a grim smile. "Then let's get to it."

The men crouched and sneaked across the blasted landscape. Cotten patted Braddock's back, pointed, and sent him on his way. Then he led Charlie toward the entrance and stopped as the cover thinned.

"We wait here," the Scout said.

They lay in an abandoned foxhole and waited for dawn to bring Fifth Fleet's invasion. In hours, thousands of Marines would storm the beaches. Charlie looked up at the stars glimmering through a veil of smoke and radiated heat, praying Fifth Fleet didn't shell the hill again before dawn.

The breeze brought a lilting sound. He caught a snatch of song. The Japanese soldiers were singing in the bunker. Despite the savage bombardment, their morale had held. They'd fight tomorrow.

"I don't know how you do it," Charlie said. "This line of work."

"I could say the same about you," the Scout said. "I hate being underwater. It was a relief to get off that goddamn boat."

Charlie smiled to himself. He hated it too. "Can I ask you something?"

"Shoot."

"What do you think it'll be like to go home when it's all over? After everything we've seen and done?"

"You mean do we deserve bein' around normal folk again."

Ever since Charlie had returned to duty, the headaches had stopped. The fogginess and dark moments. He was back where he belonged.

"Something like that," he said.

"They're the ones I'm fighting for," Cotten told him. "My family. Every day, I feel like I'm fighting my way back to them."

Charlie thought of Walsh's final message, *gado*. Why. Why was he here, what was he fighting for, why did he die.

In the morning, Saipan's beaches would become a meat grinder. The Marines would work their way down cargo net ladders, pile into landing craft, and race through ranged artillery fire. Once they hit the beaches, thousands would die on both sides. Thousands of lives extinguished forever while the survivors wondered why they'd lived when so many others died.

Why were they here? What were they all fighting for?

Charlie didn't think hate was the answer. He'd met only two men who hated the Japanese so much it was their main reason for fighting. Moreau, Reynolds. There was plenty of hate to go around, but it wasn't enough for most men. Maybe enough for a battle, but not for a war.

No, they fought for love. The same reason Smokey died back at that river. The same reason Charlie was here now. So other men might live and one day go home.

"You told me you signed up to see what you were made of," Charlie said. "It was the same for me. It's not why I'm fighting now, but it was why I wanted to fight."

"And how did it work out for you?"

"I'm still here."

"I mean did you meet that guy? See what he's made of?"

"I did," Charlie said. "And I like him. That's the problem."

"So it ain't about if you can go home, but if you want to. Combat is a seducer. Every part of you sings in combat. You live completely in the moment. You face death and survive. It promises, if you survive this, you'll live forever."

"One thing is for sure. You stay out here too long, it'll break you."

"Like your crazy captain?" the Scout said.

Charlie said nothing. As much as he liked Cotten, he wasn't Navy. *Sandtiger*'s problems were family business.

Cotten said, "Every man's different. You ain't him."

The sky had become pale. Charlie tensed, feeling exposed on the hill.

"Right now, I have bigger worries," he said.

The bombardment stopped, leaving a ringing in his ears.

D-Day.

A wave of carrier fighters and bombers zoomed over the beach, strafing and pounding the ridgeline about a mile inland. A shroud of smoke and dust hung over the entire island from the previous day's bombardment. Smoke plumes rose from still-burning fires. Tracers streamed into the sky from AA batteries on Mutcho Point.

The Scout trained his binoculars at the distant water. "We got the best seats in the house for this show."

"What do you see?"

"The fleet is launching the LVTs. Here, take a look."

Cotten handed Charlie the binoculars, and he focused them on the distant American warships stationed outside the western shore's barrier reef. The massive fleet extended as far as he could see, an impressive display of power.

Light gun boats strafed the beach with rockets.

Hundreds of armored tractors and landing craft plowed the lagoon's brilliant blue waters, carrying thousands of Marines toward Saipan's beaches. A vanguard of amphibious tanks thumped suppressing fire from 75mm cannons.

Geysers of water shot into the air around them as the Japanese opened up with artillery and mortars.

Then the Meteor roared.

The shell screamed across the sky and splashed near an amphibious tank. Thirty seconds later, it fired again. The tank flew apart in a massive geyser.

Cotten sprang to his feet and charged. "'Remember!'"

Charlie chased after him. A shadow flickered across the hill as a carrier plane buzzed overhead. A distant tremor rippled through the hill. The Meteor fired with a startling boom. He spared a glance at the lagoon and saw a landing craft rise from the water in a flash of light, belching men engulfed in flames.

Time slowed; he saw everything with perfect clarity, sweeping impressions like snapshots. Now that he'd reached his goal, the long terror of the mission left him. His blood up, elation filled him. He was ready to fight. He wanted to fight.

They sprinted to the camouflaged bunker door as another plane buzzed overhead. The gun was attracting attention. Cotten prepared a two-block satchel charge. The Meteor roared again at the approaching amtracs.

"Wait." Charlie tried the handle. The door opened a

crack before he released it. With all the excitement, the Japanese hadn't secured it.

The Scout grinned. "Sometimes, you get lucky—"

A muffled crash shook the bunker, spewing a cloud of dust rolling downhill. Braddock had just dropped his surprise on the gun crew.

Cotten pulled the fuse on the charge and counted down.

Charlie opened the door as the Scout tossed it and jumped aside.

BOOM

The thick metal door flew off down the hill. Cotten charged into the thick dust cloud. Charlie followed with his Thompson.

An unarmed Japanese soldier staggered toward him, bleeding from his ears. His head pitched back as Cotten shot him with his M3 grease gun. The Scout put another round into the second machine gunner as he tried to crawl to safety.

Charlie followed him to an intersection. The Scout waved to the right and continued forward through the crew's quarters toward the gun room. Charlie broke off and followed the other corridor toward the magazines.

Cotten's grease gun fired a series of muffled bangs. Charlie rushed into the first magazine room and collided with a khaki figure coming out. He fired his submachine gun wildly into the man, who twitched in a spray of blood and collapsed. Panting, he scanned the room for more targets. Aside from neatly stacked shells, it was empty.

Charlie sprinted back to the main corridor as soldiers ran out of the other magazine with bayonets fixed. The Thompson bucked in his hands. The men in front stiffened and fell with smoking holes in their chests. The rest retreated shouting. Charlie surged forward and chased them into the narrow corridor.

A rifle cracked. The bullet hummed past his ear and ricocheted off the concrete wall behind. The soldier in front of the line yanked on the bolt of his rifle to chamber another round while his comrades shouted and tried to get a shot.

Charlie walked forward firing in bursts, dropping one man after the next until they lay stretched in a bleeding pile. Even then he kept firing until his gun clicked dry.

"Friendly on your six, sir," Braddock said behind him.

Charlie released the empty magazine and reloaded then rushed into the gun room. He found Cotten panting with his grease gun in one hand and Colt .45 in the other. A tangle of broken bodies lay strewn across the floor.

The satchel charge had blown them apart. Cotten had put down the rest.

Braddock surveyed the damage. "Holy shit."

The Scout spat on the floor. "Let's blow this goddamn gun and go home."

Working together, they reduced the barrel elevation as low as it would go. After Charlie opened the breech,

Cotten and Braddock dropped in incendiary grenades. He slammed it shut as the grenades flared and burned at 2,000 degrees, hot enough to eat through steel.

Charlie deflated as his killing rage evaporated. He stumbled outside and gazed across the shattered landscape. The amtracs reached the beaches, unloading thousands of Marines who ran through ranged mortar fire. Vehicles plowed into the palm groves, shooting at anything that moved. Tracers from Japanese MGs streamed toward the beaches from the ridge. Tiny green figures sprawled on the sand. Charlie watched it all, feeling numb.

Braddock and Cotten joined him outside. The Scout set up the radio. Braddock slumped on the ground and winced at the pain in his arm.

"Sierra Tango, this is Able Sugar, radio check, over," Cotten said into the SCR-300 handset. "Come in, over."

The Scout offered it to Charlie. "It's your pal Rusty. He's reading us five by five and asking us to send. Tell him the good news."

Still reeling from the quick fury of combat, he took the handset. His body trembled with excess adrenaline. It had all happened so fast, so unlike his submarine battles, where combat went on for hours.

Was it really over? Had they really done it?

Charlie said, "Target destroyed. Say again, target destroyed."

CHAPTER TWENTY-SEVEN
ESCAPE

Charlie gazed through a haze of smoke at the combat raging down on the beaches. Gunfire crackled as thousands of Marines assaulted the battered Japanese positions along 4,000 yards of shoreline stretching from Agingan Point to Garapan. No way to tell who was winning.

"It's not our fight anymore," Braddock said. "We're done."

"I guess that's it then."

"Now how do we get the hell out of here? What's the plan?"

Cotten was scanning the island with his binoculars. "The original plan was to get out the way we came."

"The original plan was based on getting out before the invasion," Charlie said.

"That's right."

"So what are our options now that it's started?"

Cotten lowered his glasses. "I can see a Jap gun from

here. Shooting at our guys on the beach. I say we call it in and let the Navy take care of it."

"And then what?" Braddock said warily.

"Then we do our duty. Keep spotting until the front line pushes its way here."

"And if the Japs come along first?"

"We try to make it to our front line."

"That's the problem with getting a tough job done," the sailor growled. "Somebody higher up always volunteers you for another."

Charlie said, "Yeah, well. There's a war on."

Cotten pointed out the gun and guided Charlie's focus until he spotted it. The artillery piece was barely visible under camouflage netting.

"Got it," Charlie said.

He took out his compass and moved along the hill to shoot an azimuth, or the horizontal angle measured clockwise from a north baseline. Cotten did the same. The rest was geometry. The juncture of these azimuths was the target.

The Scout raised the *Sandtiger* and requested a fire mission. He passed on the grid and direction and signed off.

"This could take a while," Charlie said. "The boat has to radio Pearl, which then has to radio the fleet."

With Cotten's binoculars, he watched Fifth Fleet's battleships while the battle continued to rage along the shoreline. The Marines were making progress.

A puff of smoke.

"Shot out!" Charlie said.

He swiveled and fixed his glasses on the target as a salvo of shells struck the earth south of the Japanese gun.

"Let's see, Charlie." Cotten took the glasses. "John, get on the horn with your boat. Request ships adjust fire. Over, fifty right. Left 150, drop 200. Fire for effect."

The second salvo pounded overhead. The shells struck the ground near the gun and exploded in a fireball that mushroomed into a massive plume of smoke.

The Scout grinned. "End of mission. Target destroyed."

Braddock relayed the message. "Well, that was fun. What's next?"

Cotten grimaced. "We got company."

A line of open-top, two-ton trucks lumbered through the hamlet of Fina Sisu and rolled to a stop at the base of the hill. Khaki-clad figures climbed out and began to toil up the slope. A platoon, around fifty men.

"They triangulated our radio signals?" Charlie wondered.

If so, the Japanese were better than he thought. Even in the confusion of the invasion, they'd detected the Americans on the hill in short order.

"They're reoccupying the hill, which is valuable real estate," Cotten said. "But it don't matter why they're here. We got Japs in the open."

Charlie ran across the hill, shot the azimuth with his compass, and rushed back shouting the number.

"Fire mission," the Scout told Braddock, who relayed the message along with the coordinates to the *Sandtiger*. "Jap platoon. Fire for effect."

"Shot out," Charlie said.

The shells struck the earth in a burst of fire and hot metal that incinerated two of the trucks and ripped apart a dozen men.

The rest charged, firing as they ran. Bullets snapped in the air.

Cotten shouted new coordinates then bolted down the hill toward Lake Susupe. "We're bugging out! Let's go!"

Braddock lurched down the hill after him. He struggled through tall grass. "Grass cut me!"

"Sword grass," Cotten yelled. "Keep moving! We got incoming!"

"Even the fucking grass is trying to kill us—"

The top of the hill exploded behind them in a massive eruption of dirt and dust. The ground jumped beneath them and flung them bouncing down the slope.

The men got back on their feet and staggered into the thick marsh. The ground cover enveloped them. Ferns, cane grass, bamboo, and reeds. Ironwood trees soared out of the wet soil. Clouds of mosquitoes swarmed around their faces.

"You want to know why I hate everybody?" Braddock was ranting. "Why I think the whole world's a bunch of assholes?"

"Not right now, I don't," Charlie said.

"It's because some rich assholes started a war! They started a war and sold it to a whole other bunch of gullible assholes, who sailed halfway around the world to kill each other in some fucking jungle!"

Charlie's boots sank into mud that grew thicker and wetter with each step. "I think we're close to the lake—"

"And then earnest assholes like you come along thinking it all means something! You can't wait to throw your life away for some made-up bullshit and drag the rest of the assholes along with you!"

"Can't you shut him up?" Cotten said.

"I climbed a cliff so I could get chased around by Japs, shot through the arm, and get my face cut up by goddamn grass," Braddock raged. "Then I blew up a bunch of Japs in a bunker and watched another thirty of them get blown sky high!"

"You're gonna get us killed next if you don't shut it," the Scout growled.

"I just killed fifty people. How is that normal? I joined the submarines so I wouldn't have to see who I was killing! I'm sick of this shit!"

"Me too, pal," a voice called from the ferns.

They froze.

"Stay just like that," another voice said. "You move, you're dead."

Soldiers emerged from the jungle around them.

Charlie peered down the barrel of a Garand and swallowed. "Don't shoot, we're Americans."

A grizzled sergeant stepped out of the foliage cradling a Thompson. "Able Company, First Battalion, Twenty-Third Marine Regiment. Who the hell are you guys?"

THE INVASION OF SAIPAN. JUNE 15, 1944. THE GRAY-SHADED AREAS SHOW THE EXTENT OF THE ADVANCE ON THE FIRST DAY.

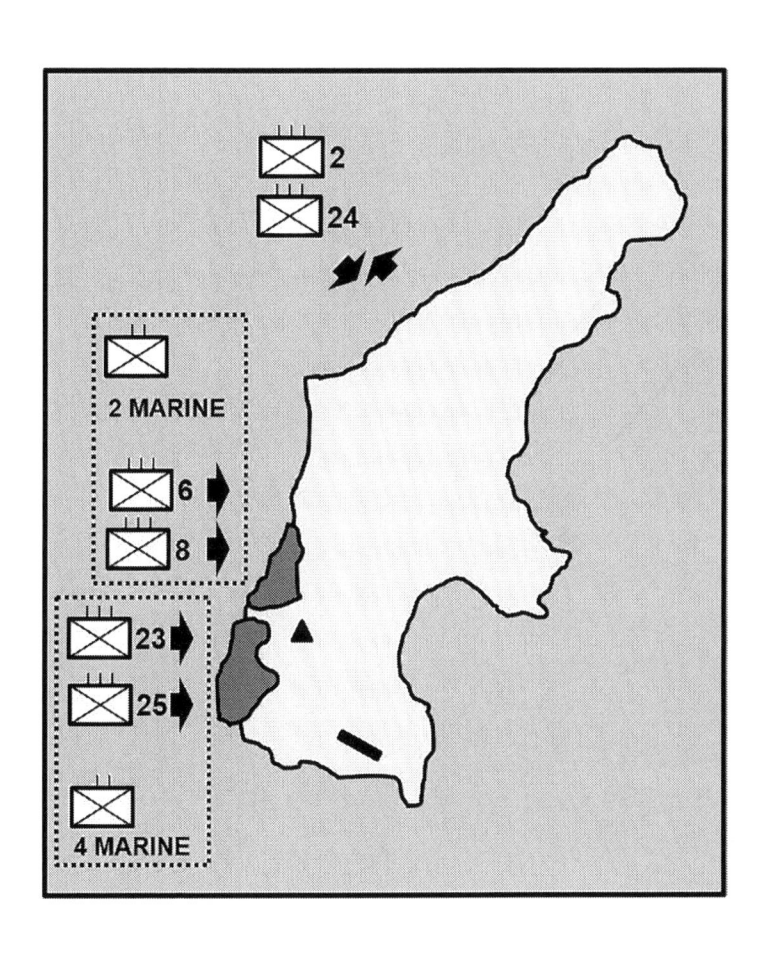

CHAPTER TWENTY-EIGHT
BACKS AGAINST THE WALL

The patrol raced from the marshes across the smoldering ruins of a cane field. Beyond, the Marines had dug in along the outskirts of Charan Kanoa, now burning under a massive cloud of dust and smoke.

Helmeted heads popped up from foxholes as Charlie, Braddock, and Cotten passed. Artillery shells howled through the air and crashed in the town.

The sergeant dropped Braddock into a foxhole so a medic could check him out. His lieutenant shouted something at him and pointed.

"Come on," the sergeant said to Charlie. "I'll take you to Captain Spencer."

Charlie and Cotten ran after him until stopping at a train of railroad cars lined up near a sugar mill, where Able Company had set up its headquarters. The cars were full of sugarcane. The tracks led past the mill into the jungle.

The captain yelled into his radio, "We're not giving

them a goddamn inch, you hear? Out!" Then he hung up and glared at Charlie. "Who the hell are you?"

"Found these guys in the swamp, sir," the sergeant said. "Some kind of commando unit. Lt. White told me to bring them your way."

Cotten sketched a salute. "Lt. Jonas Cotten, Alamo Scouts. We were assigned to destroy a big coastal gun in a bunker up on Fina Susu. Then we spotted for the Navy until the Japs sent a platoon up the hill after us."

"Uh-huh," Spencer said. "What do you want from me?"

"We accomplished our mission. We're trying to get off the island."

"That's a no go, Lieutenant. The Japs are throwing every shell they got at Charan Kanoa and the beaches. They got us zeroed, and we can't retreat. As soon as they get their shit together, they're gonna try to push us back into the sea."

"What's our options then?"

"You can pick your ground and fight alongside us, or you can take your chances," the captain said. "I don't give a crap."

"Come on," the sergeant said. "I'll take you back to my unit. We could use the help."

They dashed back to the foxholes and threw themselves into one. Two Marines were already in the hole.

"Getting crowded in here," one growled.

"Shut up, Cook," the sergeant said.

The Marine blanched as a mortar round whistled and

exploded fifty yards away. An artillery shell screamed overhead.

The sergeant cupped his hands and shouted at the distant treeline, "Is that all you got, you yellow sons of bitches?"

"That'll show 'em, Sarge," Cook said.

"The name's Vaughn," the sergeant told Cotten. "Doug Vaughn."

"Pleased to meet you, Sergeant."

"Welcome to hell. Our amtrac got bogged down 150 yards off the beach. The Japs had these little flags set up for ranged artillery. Amtracs and tanks knocked out left and right. We waded ashore and ran into barbed wire, trenches, MG emplacements. We lost a lot of guys on that fucking beach."

"Next thing you know, we're walking through a village out of a storybook," Cook said. "Flower beds and bougainvillea trees."

"Yeah, well, it's gone now. Blown to hell. You say you're Alamo Scouts? How'd you get here?"

Cotten jerked his thumb at Charlie. "He gave me a ride on his submarine."

"Now I know you're not Jap spies. Nobody would make up as crazy a story as this." He squinted at Charlie. "Submarine, huh? So you're a sailor?"

"I'm the XO of the *Sandtiger*, Sergeant," Charlie said.

Vaughn laughed. "Boy, you are out of your element now."

Charlie scanned the ground out front past the still-smoking cane field. Sparse jungle, a pig farm. "The captain seems pretty sure the Japs will attack."

"Because they will. If our planes spot their guns so our big ships can take them out, we'll advance. If not, we stay dug in while the rest of our men get ashore. Either way, the Japs are gonna try to throw us off their shithole island."

Charlie glanced at Cotten, worried he would see a job opportunity in finding the enemy spotters. The Scout nodded but otherwise said nothing.

"So we sit here and get pounded until they attack," Charlie said.

"That's right," Vaughn said.

"Tonight," Cotten said. "That's when they'll come."

"Yeah. That's when they'll do it."

A mortar round thudded into the earth and showered earth on the foxhole. Charlie flinched and spat dirt crumbs. This was too much like being depth-charged. He felt safer surrounded by hundreds of Marines, though he was hardly safe.

Actually, this was the fire after the frying pan.

A Marine brought two helmets for him and Cotten before scurrying off. Charlie took off his cap and put it on. Again, he found himself wearing a piece of uniform donated by a dead man.

The sergeant pulled a wilted pack of Lucky Strikes from his breast pocket and offered it. "Cigarette?"

Charlie didn't smoke. He'd always seen it as a dirty habit. "Yeah." He took one and bent so Vaughn could light it. Took a puff and coughed. "Thanks."

"Don't mention it. I made sure to bring a lot of smokes. There's no telling how long it'll take for the PX to get set up."

Another mortar round fell. Braddock howled from the next foxhole, "Fuck you, Japs!"

The Marines let up a ragged cheer. The sailor turned to Charlie and winked.

Vaughn shook his head. "So what's up with that guy? The big guy who was yelling his head off?"

"That's Braddock," Cotten said. "He's Navy too. Don't pay any attention to him. He went off his nut."

"Yeah, that's what worries me," the sergeant said. "He was starting to make sense."

"He did his duty." Charlie blinked at the nicotine head rush. "But like you said, we're out of our element here. He's an engine snipe."

"What's that?"

"He keeps the boat's engines running. Damn good at it too."

"I'll be damned. Is this how you guys normally do things?"

"My team was wiped out," Cotten said. "These boys chipped in."

Vaughn caught the look on his face and turned away. "Well, I'll bet you got some stories to tell."

"Some," the Scout said. "But none worth reliving."

Charlie remembered his first patrol aboard the S-55 in the Solomons. Envying Rusty for surviving the bombing of Cavite. Listening to the crew talk about how they'd survived the horror. Wanting to confront and survive that horror himself. Wishing he had his own stories to tell. Eager to earn them.

He'd never imagined some stories became a burden. That some stories could never be told and would have to be forever buried.

The shelling lasted through the day. Four dead, nine wounded. After sundown, it went on and on. Charlie slept fitfully in short stretches, jerked awake by explosions. As the night stretched on, the barrage trickled off.

Replaced by an ominous, deafening silence.

Vaughn said, "They're coming."

CHAPTER TWENTY-NINE

ALAMO

Rifle fire erupted at the sugar mill. Dozens of muzzle flashes in the dark. The popping ramped up to become a single rolling roar.

"Pull back the OPs!" Lt. White bellowed.

Marines manning the observation posts sprang to their feet and dashed pell-mell back to the foxholes dotting the jagged front line. Charlie ran over to Braddock's foxhole and jumped in.

"You all right, Braddock?"

"It's touching how you worry about me, sir. My arm is stiff as hell."

"I'm more worried about your head right now."

"In the land of the blind, the one-eyed man isn't king," the sailor said. "The blind all call him crazy."

"What about the land of the assholes? Where do you fit in?"

Braddock laughed. "There's hope for you yet, sir."

"We made it this far. We'll get through this."

"Very comforting to hear from the guy who put me here. Thank you, sir."

Charlie shook his head. He gave up.

Braddock was one of the bravest men he knew. They had one trait in common, which was they kept their head under fire. But the sailor thought the war was crazy. They were all playing war with very real bullets.

"You can always count on me to fight like the devil," the sailor said. "It's the only way I can survive the shit you get me into."

"You're one of us now," the bazooka man next to Braddock said. "The way you bitch, we're gonna make you an honorary Marine."

Destroyers boomed out at sea. Star shells burst in the night sky, illuminating the area in stark contrast of light and shadow. The gunfire at the sugar mill intensified.

Figures moving in the trees.

"Wait for it," Vaughn called from his foxhole.

Whistles shrilled in the jungle, officers signaling the attack.

"Here they come!"

Japanese infantry ran from cover in their khaki uniforms, waves of men bristling with bayonets.

"*BANZAI!*"

Their tactics favored bayonet charges, which proved effective in China. The idea was to accept huge losses for a decisive win against disorganized defenders. In this case, drive the Americans back into the sea and destroy them. Sometimes, when all hope was lost, they launched a *banzai* charge. The same thing, only the objective was to inflict as much damage as possible before dying.

Right now, the difference didn't matter. Either way, they were coming.

The Japanese fired and reloaded as they charged, flashes winking across the front. A man screamed for a medic. Confident of his shot, a Marine fired his Garand from the foxhole on the right, dropping a distant figure. Then the entire front opened up. Another salvo of star shell burst overhead.

Palm trees crashed to the ground as a big vehicle growled out of the jungle. The Type 95 *Ha-Gō* light tank opened fire with its 37mm main gun. Tracers streamed from its MG. The captain stood proud in the turret. Infantry clung to the handrails. A bugler called the charge.

Dozens of figures dropped as the charge rolled across the cane field toward the American positions. Braddock opened fire with his BAR, knocking men over like bowling pins. Charlie shouldered his Thompson and emptied his magazine, taking out two. The bazooka team fired at the approaching tank. The missile streaked through the air and missed, bursting in the jungle beyond.

"You jarheads shoot like my XO," Braddock said.

"Shut up, pipe rat," the bazooka man growled.

An antitank shell burst through the *Ha-Gō*'s light

armor and flew out the other side. The tank twisted and staggered on its tracks then kept coming.

The antitank gun's crew switched to HE rounds. The next shell blew the turret off. Flaming figures spilled out as the tank continued to roll forward at an angle, pumping thick black smoke into the air.

The engine exploded in a leaping fireball. The tank's lifeless hulk ground to a halt. The flames illuminated another tank rumbling from the trees behind it.

The bazooka man fired and yelled, "Got that bastard!" Then his helmet pinged as a bullet punctured it. The Marine toppled over like a marionette with its strings cut. His partner snatched up the bazooka only to be shot through the throat.

Grenades burst along the line as the armies closed to contact. Japanese soldiers ran screaming from the dust. Charlie stood and fired his Thompson into their chests as they closed. He fired until the weapon grew hot in his hands.

Braddock finished reloading. "We're about to be overrun, sir."

"Fall back."

They climbed out of the foxhole and retreated, Braddock shooting from the hip as he ran. The entire front line was either fighting hand to hand or dashing toward the next line of foxholes, the Japanese on their heels shouting their battle cries.

The battle became a chaotic slaughter lit by fires and

muzzle flashes and star shells. Hundreds of men shot at each other point blank or grappled in foxholes. Vaughn beat a soldier to death with a shovel. A Japanese officer cut a Marine in half with his *samurai* sword. A soldier waving a flag bearing the Rising Sun toppled under fire from Cotten's grease gun. Braddock roared as he fired into the charging Japanese with his BAR. Two Marines cartwheeled in a blast of mud and shrapnel. The wounded screamed in the mud.

Then the world shrank to a small circle as Charlie focused on his own survival, his hands steady as he pumped rounds into one snarling face at a time. Shooting, then falling back to reload, then shooting again until he had nothing left.

He dropped the gun, unholstered his .45, and kept shooting. Bullets hummed and snapped in the air around him. Half blinded by smoke and dust, he had no sense of the front anymore. When he ran out of ammo, he picked up a Japanese bolt-action rifle and stood ready with his bayonet.

Next to him, Braddock stopped firing.

The smoke cleared to reveal dead and writhing bodies covering the ground. Three burning tanks. In the distance, khaki-clad figures retreated into the trees from which they had come.

The sun was coming up. The attack was over. The Marines had held.

"Cease fire!" Lt. White shouted.

A scattering of last shots from Marines voicing their defiance, then silence. As the survivors moved forward, they called out for medics to attend to their fallen comrades.

Cotten approached from the smoke, his uniform splashed with blood. "You guys all right?"

"I'm alive," Braddock said.

"Charlie?"

Charlie gazed at the dead carpeting the fields. "Jesus Christ."

"The blind leading the blind," said Braddock. "Straight to the slaughter."

Mortars thumped in the distance.

"*INCOMING!*"

The men dove into the nearest foxhole as the Japanese barrage began again.

CHAPTER THIRTY
THE PRICE OF VICTORY

While Marines dashed across the field to rescue wounded comrades under continuous artillery fire, Charlie drank tepid water from his canteen and smoked Vaughn's cigarettes.

"And here we sit," the sergeant said. "Goddamnit."

Planes roared overhead, looking for the enemy guns that kept the Marines pinned down.

"The way they charged," Charlie said. "I still can't believe it."

"The idea is to scare the shit out of the enemy. Seeing hundreds of screaming Japs running at you wanting to stick you with a bayonet."

"Yeah, it worked on me."

"From what I heard, it worked on the Chinese too. But the Chinese have bolt-action rifles. We have automatic weapons. We lost a lot of guys last night, but the Japs lost far more. Arrogant yellow bastards."

"Still," Charlie said. "It almost worked. You got to give them credit."

"They don't mind throwing their lives away. They can keep doing it."

Navy ships boomed out on the sea. The massive shells flamed across the sky toward inland targets.

"Any country in its right mind would have surrendered by now," Braddock said. He looked pale and exhausted. "This whole war is pointless."

"Listen," Cotten said. "You hear that?"

Startled, Charlie cocked his head. The shelling had stopped. "We'll be out of here soon. Get a surgeon to patch up Braddock and then get off this island."

"Not me," the Scout said.

"What do you mean?"

"It's simple, Charlie. I'm gonna stay and fight with these Marines."

"We'll be glad to have you," Vaughn said. "Most of these guys are green. The lieutenant's all right, but he's green too. Nobody on this island knows jungle fighting like you do."

"Jonas, don't do this," Charlie said.

"It's a done deal," Cotten said. "I can do some good here."

"If you want to do good, go back to your unit. Keep doing missions."

"The battle is here. I'm gonna see it through to the end. I have to find Moretti."

The Marines stirred from their foxholes. Covered by their pickets, they began to collect the dead. Another company moved into the area and prepared for their next big push that would take them into the interior jungles and farmland. The immediate objective being to advance to Fina Susu and link up with Second Division, which was on the other side of Lake Susupe and its surrounding marshes.

Cotten was obviously looking for redemption. He'd crossed Saipan, destroyed a major coastal gun that threatened the landings, and spotted for artillery. He'd helped repel a Japanese counterattack. But it wasn't enough for him.

He believed he could go home, but he had to earn it.

Otherwise, he might bring home ghosts.

"You can't escape war without regrets," Cotten said as if reading his thoughts. "Even when you win. You got to pay the price for victory. You got to kill. You got to kill enough that you save far more. That's how it works."

Only in war could killing another human be as selfless as dying.

Charlie held out his hand. "You got your second chance, and you did it right. Thanks for getting us through this."

Cotten smiled and shook it. "Thanks for coming along."

"Good luck, Jonas. I hope you find your man."

"You too, Charlie." The Scout shifted to Braddock. "And you, John. Take care of him. He's an asshole, but he's your tribe of assholes. Remember that."

"Good luck to you," Braddock croaked and glared at Charlie. "Now let's get out of here, sir, before they volunteer us for something."

Charlie hoisted the heavy radio onto his shoulders and took up his and Braddock's weapons. He helped the sailor out of the foxhole.

"Any idea where there's an aid station?" he asked Vaughn.

"Keep walking south," the man said. "You'll find something."

"Good luck to you too, Sergeant."

Charlie led the way, Braddock lurching after him and wincing at each step. Gunfire crackled in the distance as Fourth Division pressed the Japanese.

A plan formed in his foggy brain. Get Braddock some medical attention, radio the boat, catch some sleep until they could be picked up.

At last, he caught sight of hospital tents set up next to a bombed-out building. Jeeps and ambulance trucks drove up to discharge wounded before speeding off.

Charlie went inside and instantly regretted it.

Screaming men lay on cots and stretchers. Gaping chest wounds, shattered limbs, horrifying burns. Doctors, nurses, and medics roamed among them, triaging them for care. Charlie reeled at the stench of blood, shit, and death.

He found Braddock a spot to sit and dumped their gear. A nurse hurried past; he touched her arm and asked for help.

The woman turned and stared at him, her mouth a wide *O*. He stared back.

"You," he said.

Her pretty face warmed into a smile. "Come to buy me another drink, sailor?"

CHAPTER THIRTY-ONE

AN OLD FRIEND

Exhausted and filthy, he could only gape at her dumbly.

Jane cupped his stubbled cheeks in her hands. "Oh, Charlie Harrison. Look at you. What are you doing here?"

"Special mission," he managed.

"Are you all right? Are you wounded?"

Charlie pointed to Braddock slumped on the ground. "He's one of mine."

"*Sabertooth* still?"

"No, the *Sandtiger*. I'm XO."

"Very impressive." Jane crouched next to Braddock and examined his wounds. "No major damage to blood vessels. No infection. I'll patch him up myself. Let me get my equipment. I'll be right back."

"Thanks," Braddock said.

She returned with a tray and handed it to Charlie. "You're my assistant now."

He watched her while she worked. "What you doing here?"

This was a Marine operation, Jane an Army nurse. He expected her to be following MacArthur as he hammered his way across the Solomons.

"I'm a war hero, Charlie," she said. "I found that out when I got back. I'm a nurse who survived the Philippines and came back on a submarine that sank an aircraft carrier. They had me and the girls tour around to help sell war bonds."

"Ow!" Braddock snarled.

"That's just the anesthetic, you big baby. Anyway, Charlie, when that was over, they asked me where I wanted to go."

Charlie grinned. "And you wanted to go where the action was."

"That's right." Jane poured iodine over the wounds. "You'll have some lovely scars to impress the girls back home with."

Braddock waggled his eyebrows. "Are you impressed?"

"I sure am, sailor. It's a very manly wound. In all my days as an Army nurse, I've never seen a wound like it."

"Then you should marry me, doll."

Jane laughed and glanced at Charlie. "I'm afraid my dance card is already full, big boy."

Charlie blushed as she took up her needle and thread. Braddock looked away, apparently sickened by the sight of himself being stitched up.

"Big baby," she repeated. "Since you're a friend of Charlie's, I'll give you extra stitches." She glanced at

Charlie again. "Maybe you should stay here and rest a few days."

"We have to get back to our boat," Charlie said.

"Duty calls." She cut the thread. "Good as new."

"Thanks, Jane."

"Speaking of duty calling, I can't stay and talk. There are more wounded coming in than we can handle. Maybe I'll see you tonight if I can get a break and you're still around?"

Charlie blushed again. "I'd like that."

"I can't believe I got the chance to see you again, Charlie."

"I'm glad you did."

"If I don't see you before you leave, well …" She blew him a kiss.

Then she rushed off with her tray, pausing to throw him a final glance over her shoulder before she was sucked into the frantic activity of saving more patients.

"I remember her from *Sabertooth*," Braddock said. "When we had that outbreak of meningitis. She's one tough broad."

"Yeah," Charlie said. "She's special, all right."

"If you don't marry her, you're crazy."

"Thinking about the future is a luxury," Charlie told him and went outside.

He set up the SCR-300 and hailed *Sandtiger*.

The radioman said, "Reading you five by five, Sierra—"

"Send it, over," another voice took over. It was Rusty.

"We're at an aid station near Charan Kanoa," Charlie said, providing the coordinates. "Request evacuation, over."

"We can pull you out at 2300. Be ready, over."

"Roger that, over."

"How are you? Over."

Charlie took stock of himself but still didn't know how to answer. "Ready to come home, over."

"Can't wait to see you safe and sound, brother. Over."

"You'll never guess who I just saw. Jane Larson, over."

Rusty laughed. "Remember how we used to talk about destiny? I think destiny really likes to mess with you. Over."

Charlie smiled. "See you soon, Rusty. Out."

"I'll keep the coffee hot for you. Out."

He went back inside and watched the shouting doctors and nurses work to save lives. He spotted Jane several times, once holding down a crying private while a grimacing surgeon sawed off his leg above the knee.

He bummed a cigarette and went outside. A column of Marines tramped past on their way to the front. They eyed him curiously, wondering what he'd done and seen. Perhaps envying his battlefield experience.

What I've seen and done doesn't matter, he thought. *You'll see and do plenty yourself before this battle is over. You'll have your own stories, some worth reliving, most probably not.*

If they survived. Many of them wore hangdog

expressions, knowing they might not make it back.

Charlie surveyed the aid station and smoking terrain and Marines, and he knew he'd take it all home with him. It would never die as long as he lived. For him, the war would never end.

As night fell, he scrounged up some rations and checked on Braddock. The big sailor lay sleeping on the ground, his good side supporting his weight.

No sign of Jane.

Back outside, he found her leaning against a stack of crates. She took a drag on a cigarette and exhaled a long stream of smoke.

"Can I have one of those?" he said.

She gave him one and lit it. "Smoke 'em while you got 'em."

"I didn't know you smoked."

"It's a new thing," she said. "I didn't know you smoked either."

"I saw you working in there. You were amazing. I knew after I left you at Pearl you'd want to get right back to it."

"Careful what you wish for. I flew to the front in a C47 sitting on boxes of ammo. Flew back responsible for twenty-five GIs either wounded or infected with malaria, beriberi, and other tropical diseases. My first patient had been hit in the spine and had to look forward to spending the rest of his life paralyzed from the neck down. The C47 touched down on an airstrip that was under attack by Jap planes."

"I don't know how you do it. So much blood and death, day in and day out."

Jane didn't say anything for a while. Her body stiffened, as if she were consciously holding herself together. Then she sighed it out.

She took another drag on her Lucky Strike. "You have no choice. Losing them is hard. When it gets too hard, I think about all the men I saved."

"Do you know what karma is?"

"It's a Hindu thing, right? What you do now affects what happens to you in the future."

"Like a bank, from the sounds of it. You've got plenty of it, I think. Me, if I survive this war, I'm going to have a lot to make up for."

"I'm not as pure as you think," Jane said. "I'm here to help you kill Japs. The more you kill, the faster this war is over and the killing stops."

"Yeah," he said. The idea of taking lives in war to ultimately save more lives sounded appealing to him, but he wondered if it was just something he told himself to feel all right with it. "But still. I think if I survive this, I'll become a doctor and work on getting my ledger in balance."

"I've missed you, you know," she said. "Every soldier becomes a philosopher at some point, but you're the only one I've met who really thinks about it."

Charlie looked into her eyes and turned away quickly.

He'd missed her too, as much as he missed Evie. Strange to love two women for completely different reasons. Jane understood him as a warrior, the man he'd discovered out here in the Pacific. Not surprising, as she was a warrior herself. She represented today, a present where one didn't dare dream about tomorrow, where tomorrow might never come.

Evie, however, understood him as a man. The man he was in peace, the man he hoped to become again. Gentle and nurturing, she represented tomorrow, a future where he hoped to put today behind him.

"Braddock and I are leaving at 2300," he said.

"I'm off for a few hours."

The right course was to have neither of them. Not until the fighting was done.

He said, "I should let you rest."

Her blue eyes flashed. "I'll rest when I'm dead."

Then she kissed him.

CHAPTER THIRTY-TWO
A DISTANT DREAM

The sailors hauled Charlie and Braddock aboard in moonlight.

Reeking of sweat and diesel, Rusty grinned and extended his hand. "You did it. You goddamn went and did it."

Charlie shook it warmly. "It's good to be back."

"The captain wants to see you. And I need to debrief you."

"I believe you promised me a cup of coffee."

Charlie spared a final glance at Saipan glowing red in the darkness. Cannon fire boomed as the Marines fought.

Somewhere out there, Lt. Cotten fought alongside them.

The Scout stayed to avenge his comrades, rescue his captive sergeant, and earn the right to come back. Maybe he did it for one more reason. Maybe he wanted to see it through. Maybe he stayed because he'd found himself in combat and no longer knew who he was outside it.

A part of Charlie wished he'd stayed too. Already, he missed it.

A strange feeling.

"I'm heading to my rack, sir," Braddock said. "If you need me for anything important, do me a favor and ask somebody else to do it."

The sailor lumbered down into the hatch. Charlie slid down the ladder after him into the hot and muggy belly of the beast. Red-faced and sweating, Captain Saunders leaned on the periscopes. Percy smirked at him from the plotting table. The crew at their stations.

He was back on *Sandtiger*, this hot, stinking, crowded boat with its tense crew, tedious routines, and constant work. He was home.

Braddock kept going, heading below deck for his rack time. He didn't care what the Old Man thought of the mission or anything else. Accolades and reprimands alike bounced right off him.

"Congratulations, Mr. Harrison," the captain said.

"Thank you, Captain."

"You did an outstanding job. All of you."

"I'm sorry to say we lost Chief McDonough. He died saving our lives."

"I understand," Saunders said. "Smokey knew his duty, and he did it right to the end. I'll be recommending him for the Navy Cross."

Charlie opened his mouth to tell the captain what he thought of his platitudes but checked himself. Smokey did know his duty. He understood how important the mission was. He'd given his life for it. He'd died so that other men might live.

"Thank you, sir," Charlie said.

In his way, Saunders was also telling him Smokey's death wasn't his fault. They accomplished the mission. Smokey died for it. How it all went down didn't matter. What was done was done.

"I see a long career in the submarines for you and Mr. Grady."

"Thank you, Captain," Charlie said with more feeling. He'd gone on the captain's foolhardy mission. In return, Saunders would honor his part of the deal.

"You're back just in time. Get your rest. We'll be in action soon."

"Action?"

The captain turned away. "Helm, come to two-seven-oh. All ahead full."

"Come to two-seven-oh, aye, Captain," the helmsman said.

Charlie turned to Rusty. "What did I miss?"

"It's the big one, Charlie," his friend said. "The Mobile Fleet is coming."

He couldn't believe his ears. If the report was right, this was it. *Kantai kessen*. The final battle the Japanese had planned long before they bombed Pearl Harbor.

"Show me."

At the plotting table, Rusty pointed out the *Sandtiger*'s

position and bearing. "*Flying Fish* spotted a Jap battle group coming down the San Bernardino Strait. *Seahorse* sighted another group near Mindanao." These submarines had been ordered to report enemy warship movements before attacking. "They radioed Pearl."

Charlie inspected the chart. Apparently, the enemy force was large enough to make Admiral Spruance believe he faced a major battle. Fifth Fleet was moving west from Saipan into the Philippine Sea to get maneuvering room.

Since 1942, the Americans had fought their way across the Pacific. They'd finally reached an island that put Tokyo in range of bomber planes. The Japanese had no choice but to fight now. Within the next few days, two massive fleets would engage in the largest naval battle the world had ever seen.

In tonnage, the American fleet was the largest ever assembled. While likely outnumbered in warships, the Japanese had advantages. The easterly trade winds meant Spruance's careers had to steam east to launch their planes. The Japanese would have the initiative.

Meanwhile, they could launch planes from nearby islands to augment their carriers. Their planes had a longer range.

While navies fought with guns, they also fought with airpower, which had proved decisive time and again in naval battles. The Battle of the Philippines might be fought at sea but decided in the air.

"I see the situation," Charlie said. "Where do we fit in?"

Saunders joined them at the plotting table. "Right now, we're able to act at our discretion. We're moving west, ahead of the fleet. How would you like to sink another carrier and shorten the war, Mr. Harrison?"

Charlie smiled. "I'd like that very much, Captain."

"Then get some rest and report back at 0600, Number Two."

"Aye, aye, sir."

"We're at relaxed battle stations. I'll call the men to quarters when we sight the Jap fleet."

"Come on," Rusty told Charlie. "I'm buying."

They left the conn and stopped in their cabin. Charlie peeled off his grimy commando fatigues and carefully folded them. Then he put on his service khakis, becoming a naval officer again. A great weight lifted.

In the wardroom, Charlie poured himself a mug of strong black coffee and sipped it with a sigh. Already, the horrors of Saipan seemed like a bad dream.

Rusty eyed him. "You all right?"

"Did I miss anything else while I was gone?"

"The captain got his head screwed back on straight."

"He seems rational," Charlie agreed.

"After you left, he came to his senses about sending you on that crazy mission. It had him tied in knots."

"We accomplished the mission."

"It's a hell of a thing, what you did," Rusty said.

"It cost us Smokey."

"I know. He was a good man."

Charlie stared at his coffee. "He taught me a lot about seamanship and how to read the crew. Amazing instincts. I'd always see him hard at work. He never seemed to sleep. He had a saying, 'I'll sleep when I'm dead.'"

"He's resting now."

Charlie sat at the small table and sighed. Smokey had become a memory. He'd honor it by writing to the man's family and keeping that memory alive.

"What happened out there?" Rusty said.

Charlie told him everything. As Rusty listened, his eyes grew wider and wider. One by one, the chiefs came in to hear the story until a crowd filled the small room. They were devastated at Smokey's death.

"After we left Cotten, I took Braddock to an aid station..."

In his mind, Jane smiled at him. The room dimmed.

"Percy, help me get him up," Rusty was saying.

The crowd broke up as Rusty and Percy draped Charlie's arms over their shoulders and heaved him from the chair.

Dead on my feet. Charlie had never understood that expression before now.

"I saw Jane at the aid station," he mumbled. "We were..."

His mind flashed to their kiss. The hours spent in her tent.

"I hope that sentence ends with you behaving like a gentleman," Rusty said.

Percy laughed. "You got the luck of the Irish, *Harakiri*."

They took him to his bunk and left him. Charlie curled into a ball. He twitched, jerking awake repeatedly at the nagging feeling he was in danger. Explosions flashed in his mind's eye. Then sleep overcame him.

He dreamed of screaming Japanese soldiers charging with their bayonets.

He dreamed of Jane, kissing him for everything she was worth.

He dreamed of Saipan.

CHAPTER THIRTY-THREE
KANTAI KESSEN

Charlie awoke to the battle stations alarm gonging throughout the boat.

The hard fighting and knocks he'd taken over the past few days caught up to him. His head throbbed, stabbing pain behind his eyes. He sat up groaning, rubbed his face, and checked the time.

1033! The captain had let him rest. He lurched to his feet and rushed to the conning tower. There, Percy told him the captain and Rusty were topside.

Charlie glanced at the SJ radar scope, which was clear up to fifteen nautical miles. "What's the situation?"

"Not now, Exec," Percy said and went back to talking to the bridge.

His eyes shifted to the SV radar. The skies were crowded with planes, all within six miles.

"The Japs are attacking Fifth Fleet," Nixon said. "The sea and sky were clear all around, then all of a sudden there are dozens of planes up there."

"Wait," Charlie said. "We're still surfaced."

"Yes. The captain—"

Charlie hustled up the ladder, ignoring the aches in his stiff muscles, and joined the captain and Rusty on the bridge. The men aimed their binoculars at the sky. A sailor handed him a pair of glasses.

"My God," he said.

More than a hundred planes battled in dozens of dogfights. Tracers streamed between the fighters. Bursts of black smoke.

All of it happening almost right over his head.

"The Hellcats are kicking their ass," the captain said.

Trailing a line of smoke, a spinning Japanese plane hurtled into the sea.

Rusty grinned. "There goes another one."

Charlie swept the battle with his binoculars. Tangled contrails. A plane broke into pieces. Saunders was right. The Japanese Zeros were flaming out of the sky.

Singly or in pairs, some broke free and zipped off toward the east.

"How far away is Fifth Fleet?" Charlie said.

"About seventy miles," Rusty told him.

Another squadron of American fighters, mere specks on the horizon, emerged from the blue to take on the Japanese survivors.

"I never saw anything like it," the captain said. "Our Hellcats tore them to shreds. Their Zeros!"

The Grumman F6F Hellcat succeeded the old Wildcats,

which had been chewed up by the light and fast Zeros flown by experienced Japanese combat pilots. Many of those pilots were killed at Midway and the Solomons, however. And the Hellcats flew faster, were armored, and were now flown by Americans who had gained valuable experienced in numerous combat sorties.

Charlie thought of the fierce but futile assault against the Marine line. Waves of charging Japanese infantrymen mowed down by automatic weapons. They still had fanaticism on their side, but it just wasn't enough to beat advancing American technology.

"We're better than them at war now," he said.

"Damn right," Saunders said.

He saw it. The Japanese were defeated, only they didn't know it yet.

His thoughts spiraled back to his own survival.

"Captain, that action is within six miles, and we're sailing in broad daylight. Recommend we submerge."

"We'll submerge after we spot the Jap fleet," the captain growled.

"Then what about submarines? We're not even zigzagging."

Saunders turned and gave him the stink-eye. "You want to sit this out, Mr. Harrison? Miss the *kantai kessen*?"

"No, Captain."

"Then stop suggesting we warm the bench."

"Aye, aye."

The captain was right. Getting in this game required

risk. A big risk in this case, but for the ultimate reward. If this was the final, decisive battle, every effort helped. If they could knock out an aircraft carrier, it might change the battle's outcome. If he was alive, Captain Moreau would agree with Saunders.

Saunders had called in every favor and used every bit of leverage to get this posting and have one more time at bat. Repeat the circumstances, and this time do it right. Especially today, especially this battle. He wasn't sitting this out.

Still, Charlie couldn't help but wonder about the circumstances Saunders wanted to repeat. A Japanese plane had strafed the *Flagfin* after the captain had taken a similar shortcut and exposed his boat in daylight.

That was the thing about big risks for big rewards. The risks were, well, big. For every hero who got his rewards, dozens failed and died. The storybooks told you about the knight who slew the dragon but never told the stories of all the dead knights who'd come before.

"Steady as she goes," Saunders said, which finished the conversation.

Rusty glanced at him with wide eyes. He'd reached a similar conclusion about the captain. Charlie, however, had little fight in him. He gripped the gunwale, seized by a sudden bout of nausea.

"You all right, Charlie?"

He nodded and took a few deep breaths until it passed.

Rusty added, "You might want to sit this out."

The captain lowered his binoculars and gave him a questioning look. Charlie steeled himself and shook his head. No way was he sitting this out.

"I'm all in," he said.

"You'll make a great captain of this boat," Saunders told him. "Keep yourself together and your head in the game."

"Bridge, Conn," Percy said over the bridge speaker. "Sugar Dog has picked up another wave of planes approaching."

"Thank you, Mr. Percy," Captain Saunders said. "We've got eyes on them."

Charlie raised his binoculars and spotted the massive wave of fighter planes. More than 100 Zeros and bombers. The Japanese were sending everything they had. Their objective was simple. Suppress the American fighters, sink aircraft carriers and capital ships, and sow confusion.

After that, the Imperial fleet would make its assault and finish it.

"Here come our flyboys," Rusty said.

The air hummed as the formations collided. Flashes winked across the sky. Planes circled like angry hornets. Others burned in screaming descent. Two planes cracked into each other and locked wings before spiraling into the sea.

Dozens of Japanese planes fell to the sea. It was a massacre.

"You know how you wanted to be there at the end?" Charlie said to Rusty.

His friend turned. "Yeah?"

"This might be it."

He gasped at fresh stabbing pains behind his eyes. He rubbed them. His upper lip felt wet. He wiped at it. His hand came away streaked with blood.

He wasn't well. He knew that. But he couldn't leave his post, not now.

"Plane, near," one of the lookouts cried. "Bearing two-six-oh, elevation four-triple-oh!"

Charlie squinted at the blue sky laced with contrails. A black dot grew larger by the second, taking the terrifying shape of a plunging fighter plane.

"Captain," he croaked. "Recommend we dive now!"

"Relax, Number Two." Saunders studied the aircraft with his binoculars. "It's one of ours."

"Does he know we're one of his?"

"If we dive, we'll never get another chance!"

Sandtiger flashed recognition signals at the approaching plane. The lookouts waved frantically. The air filled with the high-pitched whine of propellers.

Charlie glared at the captain. He'd bucked the man once before and nearly lost not only his own crack at command, but his career in the submarines.

If he hadn't, however, the *Sandtiger* might now be resting on the bottom of the sea, her crew on eternal patrol.

"He's not breaking off," Rusty said. "Captain!"

Saunders blinked. "Can't he see we're part of the fleet?"

"Captain!"

Charlie bawled, "Dive, dive, dive!"

The diving alarm sounded. The lookouts scrambled down the shears.

Saunders gaped at the Hellcat plunging screaming toward his submarine.

Charlie grabbed his arm and pulled. "Get below, sir! Now!"

The captain dropped into the hatch as the Hellcat's fifty-caliber machine guns raked the *Sandtiger* stern to bow. Charlie threw himself to the deck as rounds thudded around him, spraying dust and bits of metal.

The plane's shadow swept over him.

Rusty reached from the open hatch. "Come on!"

Sandtiger had begun to angle down for her dive, her decks already awash. Rusty had to close the hatch in seconds or risk killing them all.

Charlie lunged into the opening and dropped to the deck in a tumble. Above him, Rusty called out the hatch had been secured.

"Take us deep, emergency!" Captain Saunders shouted.

The crew hunched tense at their stations as the boat clawed for the depths.

"Three compartments reporting leaks, Captain," Nixon said.

"Go!"

"Aye, aye!"

Charlie tried to stand but fell back again. The conning tower spun in his eyes. Rusty helped him to his feet.

"Captain Saunders," he seethed.

The captain turned to him with wide eyes. Anger burning in his chest, Charlie started to speak but considered his words. He wanted to tell the captain he was fit to lead men into danger but no longer able to handle a crisis. That he could no longer manage the big risks required for big rewards. That he didn't care what the captain said about him or did to him; the truth was the truth, and he wasn't about to see himself or the men on this boat killed for a lie.

Saunders averted his gaze. In every aspect, a defeated man.

Charlie's anger bled from his chest.

Captain Saunders had wanted to redeem himself by repeating the crisis that had broken him, and this time doing it right. He'd failed.

"I'm sorry," Charlie said.

"Mr. Harrison, you are—"

The room spun again as Charlie crumpled to the deck. Then blackness.

CHAPTER THIRTY-FOUR
A BITTER VICTORY

Nightmares and visions.

Captain Kane said, "Very well!" just before the S-55's conning tower exploded. The Mizukaze rammed the boat with a shriek of metal. Pierced by bayonets, Reynolds plummeted over the gunwale. The foghorns of giant Japanese warships groaned in a thick mist. Sailors opened fire on Japanese soldiers flailing in the water. Destroyers and a submarine disintegrated in his crosshairs. Screaming Japanese sailors floundered in a burning oil slick.

And he was drowning as the conning tower flooded—

Charlie awoke with an anguished cry. His blurry vision cleared as he gulped ice water from a mug placed against his lips.

Then lay back on his sweat-soaked bunk and groaned. "I'm alive." He opened his eyes again. "I'm alive, right?"

Rusty wrung a cold, wet cloth and put it on his friend's forehead. "You think this is Heaven? Yeah, you're alive. You had me worried all over again."

"What happened?"

"You caught something on that island. It knocked you flat."

"I still feel like shit," Charlie said. "What did I catch?"

"Some tropical disease. You're lucky it wasn't malaria. And lucky for me, it isn't catching."

"What about Braddock?"

At that moment, the sailor knocked on the doorframe and entered. "How's the asshole doing today, Doc?"

"Speak of the devil," Rusty laughed.

Charlie smirked. "So you came to check on me."

His face reddening, Braddock thrust his hands in his pockets. "Just seeing what it is…in case I might have caught it…"

"Thank you for your concern," Charlie said with as much gravity as he could muster. "I'm touched. How's the arm?"

The big sailor stormed off. "Ah, to hell with you, sir!"

"The little things," Rusty said, still chuckling.

"Where are we?"

"About 1,500 miles east of Saipan, heading to Pearl. We'll be back at the base in less than a week. You've been knocked out for four days."

"What's the boat's condition?"

"We took a lot of damage from that Hellcat. We never did get into the battle and started home for repairs. The next day, Fifth Fleet counterattacked with aircraft and did some damage. The Japs ran turned tail after that."

"Some *kantai kessen* that turned out to be."

"It sure was!" Rusty exploded. "The brass is bragging their flyboys pretty much wiped out the Jap naval air arm. I wouldn't believe it if we didn't see it for ourselves. Plus *Albacore* and *Cavalla* sank two carriers!"

"Wow," Charlie said. "Those lucky dogs. Good for them."

"Don't worry, hero. The war isn't over yet. You'll get another crack at the Japs."

"If the captain lets me."

"I don't know," Rusty said. "He's playing it close to the chest. Quiet as a lamb. Getting shot up by one of our own planes really shook him up."

"Give me some more of that water, please."

The intelligence officer filled the mug from a pitcher and handed it to him. Charlie drained it in two gulps.

"Thanks." He groaned as he made it to his feet. "Now I'd like to get some chow and coffee. Alone, if you don't mind. I've got some thinking to do."

In the wardroom, Charlie ate everything Waldron brought out for him, replenishing consumed calories. His body trembled with fatigue. He still wasn't well. He toughed it out and went topside.

The Pacific sprawled to the horizon, calm under balmy skies. The lookouts asked him how he was doing. He answered with a thumbs up. He attached a line to a bucket, tossed it overboard, and hauled it up for a sponge bath.

For four days, he'd been in and out of consciousness

and plagued by fever dreams. Pale and thin, he sat dripping on the deck just breathing, happy to know he was still alive and on his way back to Pearl.

Now he had to think.

He'd gone against Captain Saunders' orders and dived the boat. The captain might appreciate it or want his head. No way of telling with that man. Saunders had failed a deep personal goal. The last time that happened, he'd looked for somebody to blame. Charlie and Rusty had taken the fall.

The fact was the captain had proven himself one of the great submarine aces, but the war had ground him down. He'd wanted to go out with glory, which required one final successful patrol. But he was no longer the man who'd put 39,000 tons of Japanese shipping on the bottom.

And war gave you what it gave you regardless of personal crusades.

Cooper shouldn't have allowed him to lead men into combat again. And Saunders shouldn't have asked for it. Charlie couldn't blame him for wanting it, though. If he were in the captain's shoes, he might want the same thing.

Regardless, when he saw that plane diving toward the *Sandtiger*, Charlie had to take action to save the boat. If Saunders wanted to court-martial him, so be it.

He returned to his cabin, put on his rumpled service khakis, and went to the captain's stateroom.

"Come in, Mr. Harrison," Saunders said.

Charlie entered the small room and found the captain at his desk. The man had been working on his patrol report. Charlie wondered what Saunders was writing. The backgammon game had been put away.

"Just letting you know I'm recovered and able to return to duty, Captain."

"Very well."

"Rusty filled me in on what I missed. It's too bad we didn't get our chance."

"Some regrets can't be changed," Saunders said. "We have to find a way to live with them. You would do well to remember that as you collect your own."

"Sir, about what happened when the plane came—"

"There's no need to speak of it, Mr. Harrison. Understand?"

"Yes, sir."

"Return to your duty."

"Aye, aye, Captain."

Charlie left the room a little shaken. Captain Saunders hadn't threatened court-martial, but he hadn't absolved him either.

He couldn't do anything about it.

Return to your duty, the man had said. Aye, aye.

CHAPTER THIRTY-FIVE
FINAL RECKONING

Old Glory waving from the shears, *Sandtiger* dieseled into the Pearl Harbor channel mouth. Relying on his near-photographic memory, Nixon called out bearings to navigate the channel. Dressed in white hats and dungarees, off-duty crewmen stood in neat rows on the deck. Pirates cleaned up to return to civilization.

Captain Saunders conned the boat to the Submarine Base and warped her alongside one of the piers. The Navy band struck up, "The Battle Hymn of the Republic." A small crowd cheered the submarine's arrival.

"All stop!" Charlie bawled. "Take in the mooring lines!"

Sailors on the pier hurled heaving lines onto the deck. Line handlers grabbed the ropes and pulled them in to attach them to cleats.

The captain dismissed the ship's company. The crew tramped down the gangplank to greet family and receive their mail. They accepted fresh Hawaiian fruit and ice cream cones. Charlie caught sight of John Braddock in the mob. The sailor turned and sketched a rough salute before winking and heading off to his liberty.

The gestures promised trouble but also respect.

"I'm off like a taxi dancer's dress," Percy said. "See you at the O-Club."

"Hell of a banjo player," Rusty said as the officer left grinning at the prospect of weeks of vice ahead of him. "I'll give him that."

Charlie nodded, preoccupied at the thought of facing the music. "He's a good officer. If you can get him on the boat."

"First round's on me at the Club. See you there?"

"Yeah, Rusty."

"However it turns out, the crew knows what you did, and so do I. So will Cooper. He's smart enough to read between the lines. Worst case, you might land a cushy job in San Francisco. Be near that girl you should be focusing on instead of that sexy nurse."

Charlie sighed. "Whatever the punch is, I'll roll with it."

"This war's going to be over soon regardless of what happens. The Japs are near to being licked. We'll be bombing Tokyo soon."

"Then peace."

"Then peace," Rusty echoed. "Are you ready for it?"

Charlie wasn't sure. His friend's description of taking a desk job in San Francisco sounded appealing but also made him nervous.

He didn't want to think about the future. Right now, he needed rest. Each new patrol, it seemed, depleted him more deeply than the last. At the same time, he already missed the sea.

He thought about Jonas Cotten, still fighting on Saipan and searching for his lost comrade. Rusty had contacted the Alamo Scouts and let them know he was still on the island. The Scouts said they'd handle it. They took care of their own.

Charlie hoped Cotten found his man and would allow himself to go home to his family. That he'd learned how to rest without being dead.

Captain Saunders called to him. "The jeep is here, Mr. Harrison. I'm going to submit my report to the squadron commander. You should come along."

He'd expected this. "Aye, aye, Captain."

Charlie gave his weep list to Nixon to hand off to the engineering and repair officer. Then he climbed into the jeep next to Saunders. The driver sped off across the jetty and into the base. Drab buildings amid palm groves.

He glanced at the captain's profile, but the man's taciturn expression told him nothing. For the past six days, Saunders had performed his duties professionally but otherwise kept to himself. Charlie hadn't been able to read his intentions. Right now, the captain held Charlie's life in his hand.

The jeep rolled to a stop at the headquarters building.

When they reached Cooper's office, Saunders said, "Wait here."

For an hour, Charlie stewed while the captain talked to the squadron commander. He hadn't thought about smoking since he'd returned to *Sandtiger* but now wished he had a cigarette.

The captain emerged from Cooper's office. Charlie rose to his feet.

Saunders extended his hand. "Good luck to you, son."

Charlie shook it. "Thank you, Captain."

Cooper called out, "Come on in here, Harrison."

Charlie entered and stood at attention. "Reporting as ordered, Captain."

"At ease. Grab a chair."

"Aye, sir." Charlie sat and waited, sweat already crawling down his back.

"Mindanao wasn't enough for you, was that it? You had to take part in a commando operation on Saipan!"

Charlie swallowed. "Yes, sir."

"Sometimes, I can't tell if you're brave or foolhardy, Harrison. Just like Gil Moreau. Either way, the results speak for themselves. Every action you took on this patrol was above and beyond the call of duty."

"Thank you, sir."

Now, he thought, *is when the other shoe drops*.

"I've spoken with Captain Saunders, who told me quite a story. If it didn't come from his mouth, I wouldn't have believed it."

Charlie's heart sank. "Yes, sir."

"Needless to say, this was Howard's last patrol," the captain squadron commander said. "He deserved his last shot, but he's a dog that's been in too many fights. He highly recommended you take command on *Sandtiger*'s next patrol. I heartily agree. You earned it. *Sandtiger* is yours."

Charlie sat back in his chair. "Thank you, sir."

"You can thank me by sinking Jap shipping, Mr. Harrison."

"I won't let you down."

Cooper eyed him. "No. I have a feeling you won't."

Charlie left the man's office in a daze, barely remembering his exit. He'd finally reached his goal of becoming captain of his own fleet submarine. His mind swirled as it digested this fact.

He knew where he wanted to go. He started walking toward the nearest beach. Along the way, he thought about his good fortune and wondered if he deserved it. Would he be as controlled as Kane? Persistent as Hunter? Bold as Moreau?

Stubborn, like Captain Saunders?

He was now a submarine captain with all the power, responsibility, and pressure that entailed.

Careful what you wish for!

In war, men paid a personal cost to benefit those for whom they fought. Often, as in Smokey's case, victory demanded the ultimate price. For some, however, victory delivered a special reward. War had a way of grinding a man down until he broke, but Charlie wasn't broken. He'd go on fighting. Like Rusty, he wanted to see it through to the end. All the way to Tokyo.

Charlie reached the beach and walked to the water's edge. He remembered coming to this very spot after his meeting with Admiral Lockwood, back in '42. After his first submarine patrol, he'd returned to a promotion and had contemplated his destiny. His willingness to find it.

Instead, it seemed, it had found him.

NOTES ON FICTIONALIZATION

This story is based on historical events that are fictionalized for storytelling. (Including the *Sandtiger*'s near fatal run-in with a hot torpedo, loosely based on a real event that occurred aboard the USS *Seadragon*.) There are several cases where the novel significantly diverges from history, however.

The naval bombardment lasted two to three days, not one as in this book, a decision that allowed the story to keep moving. The timing of this and other major events in the book are roughly compressed for effect.

Mount Fina Susu is placed on different locations depending on the map—either just northeast of Lake Susupe or part of a strategically important ridgeline south of the lake. This novel places it northeast of the lake.

In this novel, the Americans believe there are 15,000 Japanese soldiers defending the island. This is in accordance with intelligence estimates at the time. In reality, the garrison was 30,000 defenders against some 70,000 Marines.

During the Second World War, about a dozen Alamo Scouts were wounded during more than 100 missions, but none died in combat. Operating deep behind enemy lines, they killed more than 500 Japanese soldiers and took sixty prisoners. They blew up supply dumps, gathered valuable intelligence, and staged rescue operations of civilians and prisoners of war.

The disease Charlie caught was dengue fever, a mosquito-borne infection active in the Marianas and other regions but not characterized until the 1950s.

NOTES ON THE BATTLE OF THE PHILIPPINE SEA

The Battle of the Philippine Sea didn't end the war, but it may have made its outcome a foregone conclusion. While the Japanese Empire preserved the bulk of its naval strength, the U.S. Navy discovered its power, which destroyed ninety percent of the Japanese carrier air arm with minimal losses.

All told, in this novel's aerial engagement and others occurring during the first day of the battle, American forces engaged more than 370 Japanese planes, of which only 130 returned to their carriers in what later became known as the Marianas Turkey Shoot. Many of the survivors in turn went into the sea with the carriers *Taiho* and *Shōkaku*, which American submarines sank. After the battle's second day, Japanese losses added up to three carriers, more than 430 carrier planes, and about 200 land-based planes.

In contrast, the U.S. Navy lost only twenty-three planes the first day, the result of American technology and pool of experienced pilots far surpassing Japan's during the course of the war. On the second day, when planes attacked the Japanese fleet, the Navy lost another some 110 planes, most of which were lost at sea because they crashed while trying to land at night or were ditched.

The Battle of the Philippine Sea did not turn out to be the *kantai kessen* the Japanese anticipated. That battle would come later at Leyte Gulf.

WANT MORE?

If you enjoyed *Contact!*, get ready for the next book in the series, *Hara-Kiri*, scheduled for publication in late 2017. In this episode, Charlie assumes command of the *Sandtiger* and doggedly takes the fight to the enemy—culminating in the decisive Battle of Leyte Gulf.

Sign up for Craig's mailing list at CraigDiLouie.com to stay up to date on new releases. When you sign up, you'll receive a link to Craig's interactive submarine adventure, Fire One. This story puts you in command of your own submarine, matching wits with a Japanese skipper …

Turn the page to read the first chapter of *Hara-Kiri*.

CHAPTER ONE
CHANGING OF THE GUARD

Captain Howard Saunders called all hands to quarters.

On the *Sandtiger*'s salt-stained deck, the crew mustered under the hot sun. Lt. Grady, Lt. Percy, and Lt. Nixon in dress whites. Sailors in white hats and dungarees standing tall in neat rows behind them.

And Lt. Commander Charlie Harrison, USN, sweltered in his high-necked white tunic while his heart hammered against his medals. Never in combat had he felt as nervous as he did now.

He filled his lungs with air and bawled, "Attennnnnnshun!"

Vice Admiral Charles Lockwood, Captain Squadron Commander Rich Cooper, and their entourage crossed the gangplank while the Navy band played "Semper Paratus" on the pier.

All hands saluted as one. The senior officers returned it. As the band finished, Vice Admiral Lockwood paraded, inspecting the men.

He paused before Charlie. "You believe in destiny, Harrison?"

"I believe in its pursuit, sir."

The man smiled. "Let's just say I thought we'd be doing this one day."

"Thank you for your faith, sir."

The admiral pinned the Navy Cross to Charlie's tunic. "Congratulations on an outstanding patrol. You seem to enjoy taking the fight to the enemy on land, but we're hoping that, with your new posting, we can keep you in the Navy a while."

Charlie beamed. "Thank you, sir."

Lockwood inspected the crew next, pausing to pin the Silver Star to Machinist's Mate John Braddock's barrel chest. The big sailor's sour expression broke into an incredulous grin. They shook hands.

Satisfied with his inspection, Lockwood returned to Cooper's side. One of the admiral's aides read aloud a letter of commendation for the patrol to Saipan, noting Chief McDonough's posthumous award of the Navy Cross. Every man would have a copy placed in his service record. Many had received their dolphins, and all were authorized to wear the Submarine Combat Pin.

This done, Charlie commanded the men to parade rest. Under his feet, one of the deadliest war machines ever built lay moored to the pier. A *Gato*-class submarine displacing 1,500 tons of water, the *Sandtiger* was over 300 feet long and twenty-seven feet wide at the beam. Six forward tubes, four aft, fitted with a complement of twenty-four fish. Her four big diesel engines drove her at a top speed of twenty knots on the surface, while her four electric motors allowed a top submerged speed of nine knots. She could dive to 300 feet and range 11,000 miles.

The Navy Yard had given her repairs and all the latest upgrades, including a fresh coat of black and gray paint, the latest Mark 18 torpedoes, a five-inch deck gun, SJ radar, and a streamlined superstructure that allowed her to sail with a minimized silhouette.

Sandtiger still had her scars, visible even with the new paint job. The Imperial Japanese Navy had mauled her more than once. Still, she'd delivered far worse than she'd gotten and survived every encounter. Her proud battle flag waved on the clothesline stretching from the bow to the periscope supports, displaying a grinning shark in a sailor's hat along with numerous patches bragging of ships sunk. Seventeen sinkings in five patrols, nearly 50,000 tons.

She still had more fights to go before this war ended.

"We are winning this war," Admiral Lockwood told the men. "But we haven't won it yet. With so much at stake, the Navy must have the right men commanding the submarines. It's a job for tough, decisive leaders. You men were lucky to have such a man in your commanding officer, Captain Howard Saunders."

Lockwood pinned the Silver Star to Saunders' tunic and shook his hand. "Read your orders of detachment, Captain."

Captain Saunders read his orders aloud and finished: "Haul down my flag."

Crewmen lowered the captain's pennant as the band flourished, ending with the crash of a gun salute. While the awards ceremony was highly formalized, the ritual of changing command was even more formal and steeped in Navy tradition. The ceremony officially transferred responsibility and authority over a U.S. warship from one commanding officer to another. All hands mustered with a clear view of the proceedings, as it required the entire crew to bear witness.

Saunders said, "I am ready to be relieved."

Captain Squadron Commander Cooper handed Charlie an envelope. "Read your orders, if you please, Mr. Harrison."

Charlie opened the envelope and found two carefully folded sheets of paper.

He unfolded the first. It showed a Varga Girl lying naked on pillows, giving him a mischievous look over her bare shoulder.

Charlie shot a glance at Rusty and Percy, who smirked while keeping their eyes fixed straight ahead.

He cleared his throat and unfolded the second sheet. "To Lt. Commander Charles Frederick Harrison, USN. Report no later than September 16, 1944 to USS *Sandtiger* at Pearl Harbor Submarine Base. Upon arrival on board, report to Howard Saunders, commanding officer, USS *Sandtiger* for duty as his relief. Then report to the immediate superior in command. Signed, Vice Admiral Charles Lockwood, Commander, Submarine Force, U.S. Pacific Fleet."

His mouth gone dry, Charlie swallowed hard and saluted Saunders. "I relieve you, sir."

Saunders returned the salute. "I stand relieved."

"Break my flag," Charlie commanded.

Crewmen raised his pennant to full honors.

"Scared?" Saunders murmured to him as the band played.

"Yes," Charlie said.

"The boat's in good hands. Do your duty and never look back. You'll do fine."

"Thank you, Captain."

"You're the captain now."

After the ritual ended with firing guns, Charlie marched forward to salute Cooper. "Sir, I have properly relieved Howard Saunders as commanding officer of the *Sandtiger* and report to duty."

Cooper returned the salute. "Very well, Captain."

Charlie turned to address the crew, the young faces of the men who'd survived the Sea of Japan with him, who'd sailed with him to Saipan. "The sand tiger is a very cunning shark, a night feeder that hunts by stealth. The Electric Boat Company built our *Sandtiger* well. She has fought hard and taken good care of us. But you are her fighting spirit. Submarining is a team sport, and I couldn't ask for a better crew. I'm proud to take command and continue *Sandtiger*'s winning streak begun by Captain Moreau and continued by Captain Saunders, whom we all wish well. As far as what comes next, I'll simply quote Captain Mush Morton: 'Stay with the bastard till he's on the bottom.' We keep doing that, we can all go home."

The crew broke protocol by erupting into a full-throated cheer.

Charlie said into the din, "All standing orders and regulations remain in effect. Mr. Grady, you may take charge and dismiss the ship's company."

The band struck up a plucky rendering of "Bravura" as the crew cheered again and swarmed below deck to the reception held in the wardroom and crew's mess.

Rusty grinned. "You ready for this?"

Charlie smiled but said nothing.

His friend changed his question to a statement of fact. "You're ready for this."

"Yes," Charlie said, surprised by a surge of confidence. "I'm ready."

"Remember what I told you. Half the job is doing, the other half is acting like you know what you're doing."

"I'll remember. Nice touch with the Varga Girl, by the way."

Rusty laughed. "Another reminder for you. You got to hang loose to make it in the submarines."

"Duly noted."

"That and to show you what we're all fighting for."

The fighting was almost over.

During the invasion of Saipan, American bombers had flown their first raid since the Doolittle raid of 1942. Nearly fifty B-29s based in India bombed the steel works at Yawata. The following month, American Marines completed the conquest of Saipan and liberated Guam. By August, they captured all the Marianas.

Now the Pearl Harbor Naval Base buzzed with news American forces had invaded Morotai and Palau islands. Soon, bombers would be able to stage from the Marianas and hit Tokyo on a daily basis. American grunts would continue battling straight to Honshu. The scuttlebutt was Taiwan or the Philippines were the next target for invasion. Taking either one would cut off the Japanese home islands from their supply of oil, rubber, bauxite, coal, foodstuffs, cloth, and other materials that fed their hungry war economy.

Meanwhile, the submarines would go on doing their part to starve the beast and shorten the war. Charlie chafed at the idea of attending the reception. He was captain now, the object of his hopes and destiny. What he wanted was patrol orders. He couldn't wait to get back into the fight and see it through to the end. He couldn't wait to see what else destiny had in store for him.

ABOUT THE AUTHOR

Craig DiLouie is an author of popular thriller, apocalyptic/horror, and sci-fi/fantasy fiction.

In hundreds of reviews, Craig's novels have been praised for their strong characters, action, and gritty realism. Each book promises an exciting experience with people you'll care about in a world that feels real.

These works have been nominated for major literary awards such as the Bram Stoker Award and Audie Award, translated into multiple languages, and optioned for film. He is a member of the Horror Writers Association, International Thriller Writers, and Imaginative Fiction Writers Association.

Learn more about Craig's writing at:
www.CraigDiLouie.com

Craig welcomes your correspondence at:
Read@CraigDiLouie.com

Printed in Great Britain
by Amazon